# Goandria:
# Visions of War

## R. Michael

To the Tudock girls
R. Michael

*To all with a creative spirit.*

# Table of Contents

# Map of Goandria

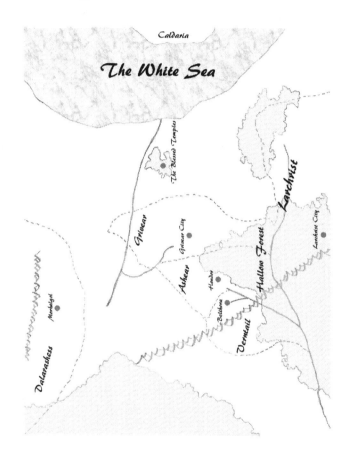

# Prologue

In the very heart of the land of Goandria, between the King and Nen rivers, ruled the Three Republics. For generations, the Republics (Verntail, Ashear, and Grivear) were spared the horrors of battle. The war between the great enemy Harkendor and the wizards had largely been forgotten.

It was an era of peace. Cities grew as armies diminished and fortresses were abandoned. There were some who did remember the stories of old, of a legendary wizard who turned against his own. There were whispers and rumors that one who brought terror to Goandria generations ago had returned. People would disappear inexplicably, some noted that the wizards seemed tense, and in the north there were stirrings of rebellion against the Three Republics. Most of the time, little faith was put in such rumors. The people of the Republics continued on in the ups and downs of life, knowing that rumors of evil wizards and witches were fairly normal. Even so, few denied there was an eeriness about the current times, for the peace they had enjoyed was short lived

From a dark, distant shadow, a man calling himself Zontose rode forth upon an armored black horse. He first took notice of a people who lived in the dense woodlands to the far west of the prosperity of the Three Republics. These people, known as thworfs, were gray-skinned, bearded, long-limbed, and perfectly adapted to their harsh environment. He witnessed their craftiness, brute strength, and savagery during the hunt, and their utter loyalty to their leaders. Smiling to himself, Zontose knew he had found what he was looking for. Riding into the thworf city, the pyramidal wooden buildings and basic but elegant huts filled him with awe. However, amidst the beauty, misery and despair were around every corner. Many of the children resembled walking skeletons, and the sick and dying were sprawled out in the streets while the elders of the community lived in luxury. Zontose conjured medicines for the sick and used his mystical powers to produce many fruit-bearing trees.

It did not take long for the elders to take notice of Zontose because the laypeople began to adore this newcomer. Feeling threatened, the elders planned to eliminate the stranger, but when they attempted to seize Zontose, the people rose up and killed their leaders. Zontose promised the thworf people that their oppression was at an end, that riches would be theirs, and that, under him, they could seize Goandria and make it their own.

With his right fist, Zontose led his thworf legions. With his left, he wielded an unholy corruption of the wizard's power. Fire and death spread unrelentingly. Village after village burned to the ground, and those who rose up against Zontose's forces became examples for all to see. The Three Republics were surrounded, trade was abolished, and crops were destroyed. Famine struck, and the kings and queens of the Republics decided war was the only course of action. Thousands of archris knights, the most elite soldiers in service of the Republics (along with what was left of the national armies of Verntail, Grivear, and Ashear) united and marched forth, meeting their greatest foe on the battlefield.

# Chapter 1

Hooves pounded into the dirt as the mighty steed carried his master home. The sun ruthlessly beat down upon the man, sweat beaded on his forehead, and his long, dark-brown hair stuck to his face. The chainmail and leather jerkin he wore beneath the armor was agonizingly uncomfortable; his skin felt like it was on fire after the long ride. A tall archway welcomed the rider as he passed through a wooden wall that surrounded the village. Rising up on the side of a hill rested the village of Fair Wood. The rider patted his horse gently. "Home at last." He sighed.

The rider inhaled deeply. His eyes twinkled as he gazed upon a familiar sight. A mid-sized, cherry red house stood out amongst the rest of the buildings. It was not particularly fancy, for it mirrored the style of the surrounding homes. Like the other houses, his was a two-level structure with arched windows that jutted out from the sides with chocolate-colored shingles layering the roof. However common the look was in Fair Wood didn't matter to the rider, for his heart leapt as he neared, and when he finally dismounted, the door flung open. A woman and a little girl ran out to greet him. An open-mouthed smile graced the girl as she giggled jubilantly.

"Aron! You didn't tell me you were coming home!" the woman exclaimed as she leapt into his arms.

"Daddy! Daddy!" the six-year-old shrieked.

Aron knelt down and hugged his daughter, running his fingers through the girl's hair and tucking it behind her left ear. A small but bright smile creased his face.

"Daddy, please stay this time?"

Aron locked eyes with his daughter. "I promise, Jori," he said, fuzzing up her hair.

Inside the house, dinner plates were scraped clean, and dishes were strewn about the kitchen. Jori ran back to her toys as Nina and Aron talked. "I'm sorry about the mess. We just got done eating when Jori insisted that we play together. It still should be hot if you would like some."

Placing his bottom in the seat, Aron let loose a relaxed sigh. A fire crackled in the fireplace, licking at the sides of the brick as it radiated comforting warmth. Candles were sporadically set around the house, providing a minimal amount of light to those inside. "Don't worry about the kitchen." He smiled. "I haven't had a home-cooked meal in ages!"

Nina strolled out of the kitchen and handed a plate of pot roast to her husband. The steaming aroma of cooked vegetables and roast beef with a side of tea made Aron's mouth water. "Mmm, looks amazing, sweetie. Thank you."

"I know your studies at the academy can be intense." Nina smiled.

"That's an understatement." Aron snorted as he packed his mouth with another fork full of food.

"I missed you, Aron. We both did. Jori kept asking me when you would come home. She just doesn't understand."

The little girl abruptly ran into the room. "Daddy, Daddy!"

"Yes, yes, yes!" Aron said merrily, scooping his daughter onto his lap. "Were you a good girl while I was gone?"

"Mhm hmm." She nodded enthusiastically.

"Daddy missed you, little sweetheart. Sorry I was gone so long."

"Were you fighting the monsters again, Daddy?" Jori looked up, her large blue eyes innocently surveying her father for an answer.

"Yes! And I drove them back!" Aron flicked his wrist, swishing an imaginary sword.

"Jori, it is time for bed, sweetie," Nina interrupted.

"Aw, but Mom, I don't wanna. Daddy is home! I want Daddy." Jori pouted, crossing her arms over her chest.

"I'll tell ya what, I will tuck you in, and tomorrow we will play."

"Okay, Daddy, but only if you promise!" Jori's large blue eyes widened.

"Of course." Aron grinned, guiding his little girl to her bedroom. Jori slowly crawled into bed, yawning so wide tears welled in her eyes.

"I thought you weren't tired," Aron laughed.

"I'm not!" Jori insisted through another yawn.

Tucking Jori's hair behind her ear, Aron sang her a short lullaby, and within a matter of minutes she was asleep. Aron bent over, kissed her on the forehead, and quietly left the bedroom. He went back to his chair in the living room.

Nina glided over to her husband and ran her right hand through his hair. "I'm sorry, Aron. I don't mean to be a nag. You have too much on your plate without me adding to it."

Aron's eyes glistened, peering up at his beloved. "I know, Nina. I understand. I wish my duties as an archris knight didn't demand that I be away from my family so long. The Three Republics are threatened, though, and the war with Zontose is not going well. His thworfs are too numerous. When the Grivear Academy doesn't deploy me into battle, they require extra training to keep me sharp. Now one of the instructors wants me to start training a new generation of archris knights." Aron sighed heavily.

"When are you returning … to the academy?" Nina's voice dropped, nearly choking on her words.

"Not sure yet. Master Epsor said he will send word when I am needed," Aron said.

"This is ridiculous! They cannot expect you to just leave on a whim!"

"Sweetie, they are my superiors. They have that right." Aron chuckled.

Sighing heavily, Nina looked at the floor. "I know, but don't they understand that you have responsibilities to your family as well? Jori needs her father, and I need my husband." Tears started streaming down Nina's cheeks. "I can't bear the thought of you fighting in this war. The Republics try to hide the truth, but it is no secret. Zontose's armies are gaining more and more footing."

Nina sat down on Aron's lap, and he held her close. "The thworf army is managing to hack its way deeper into the Republics. I am an archris knight, Nina. You do not know how much I would love to spend more time at home, but our way of life is in real danger. If the academy requires me to fight, it is just something that I must do. The Republics' army is wearing thin."

"But why do they always need you?" Nina's voice squeaked; she was still unable to make eye contact.

Aron's lips formed a tight smile, gently turning his beloved's head so he could gaze into her stunning hazel eyes. "They just do, Nina. They can't live without me." He smirked a little.

"Then I suggest we make the most of the time we have together," Nina said, resting her chest on Aron's and smiling slightly.

Morning came quickly. The wind whispered quietly through the trees, and the birds sang merrily to each other. The sun gleamed relentlessly on the village as the temperature steadily increased. Beads of sweat dripped from Aron's forehead, down his stubby beard, and onto the table surface he had been sanding. Aron glared up at the sun and grumbled under his breath. Jori sat on the ground near him, playing with her dolls, the heat not seeming to bother her.

"I don't understand what the problem is," he whined, standing to his full six-foot height.

"Are you still putzing around with that table? I thought you gave up on that months ago." his wife's voice sounded from behind.

"Yes, I thought I did, but I don't know. I figured I could try to fix it. Oh, and you will not believe who stopped by an hour ago. I have to report to the academy today. I don't get it. There are plenty of other knights off duty, and I'm sure they know more of what's going on than I do." He thrust his sword onto the newly constructed table. An instant later, the entire table collapsed.

"So what's going on here?" Nina chuckled.

"I give up." Aron exhaled deeply, giving the table a swift kick.

"Honey, settle down." Nina's nimble hands gently rubbed her husband's back.

"I'm sorry. This is just ridiculous! I was promised leave, and now they are demanding that I return to the academy. Not to mention I have to break *another* promise to Jori."

"Is there any way you could explain to your superiors that you need time with your family?"

A laugh erupted from Aron. "No, of course not. They act like none of the knights have lives outside the academy."

"Then I guess you had better get going." Nina smiled faintly as she tossed a leather jacket to Aron.

"No, not this time, Nina. I'm done abandoning my family."

"Are you sure you want to disobey your masters like that? You could get expelled!"

Aron's eyes flashed back at his wife, meeting her gaze with a quick smirk. "No, I don't think so. They need me too much."

Rapping his knuckles on a large oak table, an archris general sat alone in the war room of the Grivear Academy. He preferred to stay away from his colleagues, for he found constant military strategizing draining. Staring at the wood grain in the table, the general allowed his thoughts to run. *Where is he? It has been nearly a week. Aron should be here by now!* The thought of Aron made his blood run hot. *How dare he think that he is above listening to his superior's summons?* Taking a few deep breaths, he turned to the window behind him and gazed at the woodlands. *So many secrets forests hold, so many wonders. If only everyone here understood what was coming for them.* A small half-smile cracked the general's otherwise emotionless face. An abrupt knock banged against the door. The general rolled his eyes and prepared a fake smile as he sat down.

"Come in," the general said in a welcoming voice.

"Sir, is everything alright?" Another archris knight entered. He was a younger man with long brown hair and a short beard that covered his face.

"Quartose, what an unexpected pleasure! Do you know where Aron is? I sent for him over a week ago and heard nothing,"

"No, I don't, but last I heard, he was on leave under your own orders."

Clenching his teeth, Epsor forced a smile. "Quartose, we are at war, and that means sacrifices. Now I want Aron back at the Academy by tomorrow."

"Um … No disrespect, but why would he listen to me when he won't even listen to you?"

"Because, Quartose, you are his friend, and you will tell him that the enemy is on the academy's doorstep and we need all the support we can get."

"You want me to lie to him?" Quartose grimaced.

"As I said already, Quartose, this is war, and I want you to do whatever it takes to get him here."

Shaking his head, Quartose stepped forward a bit. "What's going on? Is he in trouble? We are not so desperate for knights that we need to resort to lying just so we can get one man back at the academy. There are other men on leave. Why don't you just send for them?"

Exhaling slowly, Epsor turned, and his eyes met Quartose's. "Do not question me, soldier. If you will not fulfill your assignment, I will find someone who can, and you will face disciplinary action for insubordination."

Quartose's heart sank. *Expulsion.* "Epsor, I have been nothing but loyal to you, to our order, and to the Three Republics. How dare you threaten me with that?"

"Your loyalty in the past will not excuse you from disobeying one of your generals who also served as your mentor and teacher. This new attitude you have is most disturbing, Quartose."

Quartose stiffened and forced his expression to change. "I will see to it that Aron is here by morning, sir."

"I knew you wouldn't let me down." Epsor smirked, turning back toward the window.

Aron could still taste the roast Nina had cooked for dinner. The savory meat cooked slowly with carrots and potatoes equaled perfection. Nothing was so wonderful to his palate. As he sat alone outside, multiple thoughts flashed through his mind. He peered toward the star-speckled night, passing a blade of grass between his fingers. Turning his gaze leftward, he saw his wife and daughter singing merry praises of joy for no apparent reason at all. They were just simply happy this night. It was way past Jori's bed time, but she and Nina got caught up in playing together. It was moments like these that Aron wished he could savor forever. Memories of a time when it was just him and his wife navigating through life, the first hut they bought to live in, their first meal together, the sheer thrill of getting to know another person. Adrenaline suddenly surged through his veins, and memories of war abruptly flashed in his mind. He witnessed fellow comrades maimed and gasping for their last breath as gloating thworf faces gleefully ended their lives. He quickly forced the memories from his mind.

Aron was not about to let this moment be ruined. Aron's ears then heard the trotting of a horse, and his heart began picking up pace as he stood up to greet the rider.

"Quartose? What brings you here at this hour?" Aron asked, reaching out his right hand in greeting.

The other man sighed heavily. "The academy needs you, Aron. We are recalling all knights to help defend it."

"Thworfs? This far into the Republics?"

Silence fell upon them for a moment before Quartose answered. "I do not know. They must have broken through our lines on the edge of Grivear. There is no time to examine the enemy's military strategy. We must hasten back to the academy!"

"Quartose?" Aron's eyes met and studied his friend's eyes. Quartose's body language betrayed him. The sweat at his brow, the short answers, the inability to maintain eye contact … "What is really going on? What aren't you telling me?"

Quartose thumbed the reins of his horse. "Nothing. Are you coming or not?"

"Let me just say goodbye to my family first," Aron answered, surveying the other for a few more moments before turning slowly toward his house.

Aron turned the knob on the door and slowly peeked in. His wife had just sat down to read a book by candlelight after putting Jori to bed for the night. Her nimble frame was swallowed up by the large chair she was in. "What's going on?" she asked, not looking up from the page she was reading.

Aron clasped his hands together in front of him, rubbing them together. "I'm not sure. Quartose says that I must return to the academy immediately. He says the enemy is nearing."

"You don't believe him?" Nina's face perked up from behind the book as she laid it down on a table next to her.

Turning back quickly to check on Quartose, Aron sighed. "Something is not right. I can tell he's lying, but I don't know why he would. Whatever the reason, it must be important."

Nina rested her cheek upon her left knuckle. "But it isn't like Quartose to lie."

"No." Aron squinted, peering back at his friend one more time. "No, it is not, but whatever it is, I can't ignore it."

Nina's nimble hand gingerly caressed her husband's arm. "Don't go, Aron."

"Nina …"

"Can't you see that something isn't right?" Nina's hazel eyes widened, meeting her husband's.

"Which gives me all the more reason to go, my dear." Aron's right hand tucked Nina's hair behind her ear.

Out of the corner of Aron's eye, he saw a small rosy face streaked with tears peeking around the corner. "Jori, you should be asleep!"

"Daddy, are you going to leave again?" The little girl's wide, innocent eyes gazed longingly up toward her father, but after a few seconds she swiftly turned back to her room, new rivulets of tears soaking her cheeks.

Aron knelt down before his daughter and dried her tears with his sleeve just before embracing her.

"What's wrong, dear?"

"The … bad man …" Jori whispered.

Aron smiled, trying to cheer her up, but inside he was worried sick about his daughter. "What about the bad man? Who are you talking about?" Aron asked gently.

"The shadow man!" Jori scowled.

Aron's heart froze upon hearing those words. Before his mother passed away, she had revealed to Aron that sometimes she would have visions of the future. She claimed that Voshnore chose their family as his personal messengers.

"Now," Aron said in a playful tone, "don't you know that your daddy will protect you against anything?"

Jori placed her hands over her face as tears flowed relentlessly from her eyes. "But you are going to leave! Don't let him get me and Mommy!"

"Jori, sweetie," Aron brushed her hair with his hand. "I would never, ever let anyone harm you or Mommy."

Jori's watery eyes met Aron's. "Really?"

"I promise, my princess. I promise." Aron held her tightly until her sobs subsided. "Did I ever tell you about the time I slew two dragons?"

Jori smiled through her tears and said, "You're just trying to cheer me up. Well, it's not gunna work!"

"I guess it will have to wait until tomorrow then."

"No, Daddy! No! See, no tears! Tell me tonight, please?"

"Alright, I'll tell you, but you must promise not to tell anyone. They might call on me to take care of their dragon problems, and I don't want to get into the pest control profession."

Jori nodded and drew an imaginary "X" over her heart.

"There I was before two monstrous dragons which held your mother prisoner. Their eyes were red with hate, and their claws were ready to rip me apart. I will admit that I was scared a little, but one thing you must remember is that fear has power only if you give it power, and your daddy wasn't going to give in to fear. Slowly they closed around me." Aron's eyes widened as he continued. "I quickly drew my sword to prepare for the fight. Inch by inch they crept forward as if they wanted to savor me and make me last for something … terrible."

Jori gasped and brought her bed sheet closer to her.

"Then," Aron's voice deepened, "out of nowhere, I see this clawed hand swipe at me. I clashed with the dragon and managed to sever his hand. But that was not enough! He began clawing at me furiously, strike after strike until eventually I hewed his left arm and struck my blade right into his belly. Yet one remained, and he was even bigger and uglier! Strike! Lightning shot from the sky," Aron went on, "and rain started falling steadily on the ground. This gave the dragon an advantage because the ground became wet and slippery, and I could barely stand to fight. Doubt was ever present in my mind; fear began to cloud my perception and dull my senses. The big dragon roared with might, thinking he had defeated his prey at last! But your father had one last trick up his sleeve. Thunder crashed in the deep, as if challenging me, telling me my efforts were in vain and that I was going to fail. I was bound and determined to not give in. I cried out and hewed the head off the dragon. After the fall of my enemy, I raced to your mother and freed her from her bonds."

"Did this all really happen, Daddy?" Jori's eyes closed sleepily.

"Every word of it is true. You see, if your daddy can protect your mother from two dragons, I can protect you from the bad man. I promise I will not let anything happen to you."

At last the little girl was sleeping. A half-smile creased her slumbering face as it rested upon a feather pillow. Aron tucked Jori's hair behind her ear then closed the bedroom door behind him.

Nina was waiting outside the bedroom in the hallway. "Did you tell her?"

Aron shook his head. "No, I managed to distract her with the story."

"Honey, we need you. Please. How am I supposed to tell our daughter you left again? She already fears you won't come back."

"I know, and we've already discussed it! I have made my decision. Do not think that it is easy for me to do this. Nina, there is more. Jori just had a dream, one like my mother used to have."

"She's a seer?" Nina gasped.

"She dreamt of Zontose."

"What does this all mean? Why does this stuff always happen to our family?" Nina's eyes began to redden again as she embraced her husband. "Do you think the Archris Knights could protect her?" Nina asked.

"I don't know, but if Zontose gets ahold of her, he could harness her power and know our attacks before we even strike. I *must* alert the academy. When I'm done with my business there, I will seek aide from the wizard order. Maybe they could help us."

Nina embraced her husband one more time and placed a tender kiss upon his lips before he turned toward the door and left the house. Nina was left standing where she was, tears streaking her cheeks while she silently prayed for her family.

Aron softly walked outside and saddled up his horse. Quartose watched his friend from atop his own steed. "Aron? Are you alright?" There was no answer. Quartose furrowed his brow, his eyes following his friend intently. "Aron?" he asked again.

"What's really going on here, Quartose?" Aron's dark brown eyes locked onto Quartose's gaze.

"I ... I am not sure; Epsor wants you back at the academy. When I questioned his reasoning for doing so, he threatened to expel me."

"Epsor?" Aron's face contorted as the question left his lips.

"Yes, now we need to get moving. I promised to have you back at the academy by sunrise."

Reluctantly, Aron agreed. The two men's horses trotted through forest and grassland, carrying their masters onward to their destination. Aron's mind buzzed with confusion on the long ride. It would take at least the rest of the night to reach the academy. Jori and Nina's faces projected themselves within Aron's mind. Aron fantasized about storming into the academy, drilling the generals for the information they were withholding, and demanding to return to his family. An entire scenario played out within his mind. He bickered with Epsor, throwing it in his instructor's face that he had never had a wife or a child before and could not possibly imagine what it was like. Aron stewed in his own situation, pondering what was going on, why he was separated from his family yet again, and how Jori was going to react when she found out Daddy had left again.

As the night passed on, Aron's mind slowly shifted. Eventually, he no longer dwelt quite so heavily on leaving his family. Images of sword and steel flashed before his mind's eye. Battles, war, fighting, death – images from the recent past Aron could not easily forget. *What is driving Zontose?* It was a simple question that weighed down his thinking. *A simple answer to that would be power. The lure of power can drive sane and normal men to do horrendous acts of evil, but I feel something deeper is driving this madman.* Flashbacks of past battles were revisited over and over by his mind's eye. An immense sea of thworfs slashing through the ranks of the archris knights, the glee that was upon their faces as they marched into battle. The thworfs' black beards were soaked in blood, hewing their enemies even after they had departed from this world. It was the first time Aron had encountered Zontose's army. In mere months, the thworf legions had carved their way through the Three Republics. The archris knights and other armies that served the Republics managed only a few minor victories, but the cost was great. Only one battle in which Aron partook was considered a victory. It was a day he would not soon forget. He was marching in the front lines, and the horde of thworfs smashed into the ranks of the archris knights, killing until they could stand no longer.

"Aron?"

Aron's eyes turned to the other rider. "Yes?"

"I wish things were different."

# Chapter 2

Sleep eluded Nina that night; she just lay in bed as her thoughts swirled. Visions of her husband fighting an endless host of thworfs, fighting until he was the last man standing upon the battlefield, fighting until the thworfs overwhelmed him, fighting until he died and could no longer set his gaze upon his family. *Aron's commanding officers have been demanding more and more out of him lately. I know that is the result of the war, but I feel like I am losing my husband. And he is missing out on Jori's childhood,* Nina thought. A couple tears streaked her cheeks, forming rivulets down her silky smooth face and ending on the pillow. A sliver of light peeked through the window. The single ray was all she needed to see: the night was at last over. Nina silently prayed as she folded over the blankets and slipped from the bed. No words left her mouth as she placed wood in the stove to heat the tea kettle, not even a good morning to her daughter who had woken just a short while before Nina. Jori smiled weakly at her mother, but Nina was in a trance-like state. Her mind screamed out to Voshnore, pleading and begging for mercy, for him to save her daughter from this terrible war and from a life where her father must always attend to duties outside the family. Nina accidentally allowed her eyes to glide across the room until they rested upon the chair Aron usually sat in, empty once again.

Then suddenly a crash reverberated through the village. Again the noise erupted from an unseen location. Nina opened the house door and stepped outside to investigate. Her heart sank and her throat tightened. A field of two-thousand swords approached in the newly risen sunlight, grasped firmly by thworf hands. Black dragons circled above as their thworf riders beat drums of war. "This isn't possible!" Nina cried out, stumbling back into the house, hastily closing the door behind her. She frantically looked around. Within a few moments the legion would be upon the city. Looking up at the ceiling, Nina prayed quickly, and then her eyes met her daughter's. Jori had stopped playing and was standing wide-eyed in the kitchen. She was a smart girl; Nina knew she was aware that something was amiss. Nina fought hard to hold back her tears as she came over and knelt down in front of her daughter. "Jori, sweetie, I need you to stay in the house and hide, hide so no one will find you! No matter what happens, do not leave this house."

"There are monsters coming, Mommy. They want to hurt us! Will Daddy save us? Where did he go?"

Nina leaned in and embraced her daughter. "Honey, how did you know about the monsters?"

"I saw them last night. I didn't think they were real. You and Daddy always tell me monsters do not exist, but when I heard the bang, it was exactly like my dream."

The stench of smoke began to fill Nina's nostrils, and the sounds of screams stung her soul. The thworfs were upon them. Nina rushed to her room and grabbed the short sword that hung on the wall. Back in the living room, she shouted back at Jori, "Hide now! And don't leave!"

"Mommy, Mommy! Don't go! Mommy!" The slamming of the house door cut off Jori's cries. She was alone. Tears filled her eyes as she sobbed uncontrollably. Her little feet carried her down the main hallway to her parent's bedroom. Heaving open the heavy, wooden, closet door, Jori stepped inside and closed it again. She piled several of her mother's dresses on top of herself as she lay in the corner.

Outside, the thworf butchers sliced their way through the village. They jeered and laughed as their swords hacked apart their victims. It did not matter to the blundering savages that merely a few were armed. Death and destruction was their goal. Only twenty-nine men had swords within the village, and a few farmers grabbed pitchforks or hunting bows when the need arose. The swordsmen met their foes, outnumbered so vastly their efforts seemed rather pointless. Still, they each took up their blades and shields, some of which were simple and makeshift, and they formed up, daring the thworf legion. Already much of the village had been slaughtered. Many were hacked to pieces by thworf swords and axes, and others were peppered with an unnecessary amount of arrows. The air stunk like death. What was once green, brown, and yellow was now one color: crimson. Nina had only one concern, and that was the safety of her daughter. Thworfs continued to swarm toward Nina, but she refused to relent. Her daughter's life depended on it. Her green dress and dark hair were bloodstained, and her arms groaned as she repeatedly lifted her blade. Flames started to lick the village. Most of the defenders had fallen, and those who attempted to flee were immediately shot with arrows. The flames rose quickly, and black smoke billowed into the air. A few people seized the opportunity to escape the death trap, but most were crippled by hacking and coughing uncontrollably.

A dozen thworfs lay dead at Nina's feet. Their comrades were preoccupied at the moment, and Nina took the opportunity to burst into her house again. Casting her sword on the ground she called out for her daughter. Nina's voice cracked as she screamed Jori's name once more. Again there was no answer. Her head quickly turned to check outside. The fire was close now, too close, and more thworfs were coming her way. "Jori! Sweetie, where are you?"

The little girl burst out of the room, running into her mother's arms. "Mommy, you came back!" Tears streaked both their cheeks as they embraced.

"We need to go, Sweetie," Nina tucked her daughter's hair behind her ear. She smiled through her tears, dried her eyes the best she could, then clasped Jori's small fingers in her own. Outside, Nina's legs carried her as fast as Jori would let them. As the village succumbed to the slaughter around them, she only cared about getting her little girl to safety. All around them the air began to get colder. Nina thought nothing of it until her sweat turned to frost.

"Mommy, it's cold," Jori remarked. Nina's eyes widened, for it was mid-summer, and the fires that ravaged Fair Wood were not far away. In the heart of the village emerged a ghastly shape. It looked like a man but taller. A black cloak was draped over its gray tunic. Nina watched as the being marched through the streets, a squad of thworfs trailing behind him. When he stopped, the thworfs obediently halted as well. Nina and Jori ducked behind a bunch of rubble. Nina peered cautiously around the corner to see what was going on. The ghastly figure looked around and then suddenly met Nina's gaze.

The sight she beheld was unlike anything she had ever witnessed in her life. Beneath the hood, nothing could be seen save for two glowing blue eyes and what seemed to be a very faint outline of a skull.

Jori tugged at her mother's sleeve. "Mommy, what is it? What's going on out there?"

"Jori," Nina said very slowly, her eyes still locked onto whatever it was she was seeing, "we need to run. That means I need you to run as fast as you possibly can." The ghastly foe began to charge right for them. "Sweetie, we need to go now!" Nina screamed. Without thinking, she scooped up her daughter and turned to run back the way they had come, trying to find a different way to escape the village. The figure in the black cloak drew his weapon: a strange sword that was bent slightly and serrated on half. He was quickly upon his prey. Nina felt a sharp pain in her right shoulder. Crumbling to the ground, she gazed upward at her assailant. The dark one's sword tip was stained with blood, and his hypnotic eyes bore into Nina. They did not move or pivot, just stared into her. She felt as if he could see her very soul. After a brief silence, the ghastly being spoke. "Bind the girl; kill the mother."

The sun had at last begun to peek over the horizon. Early morning had come. The bright, yellow-orange rays glittered off the clouds, turning them to violet, red, and pink. In the distance arose the Grivear Academy. Aron's heart pounded faster at the sight of his school. Nervously thumbing the reins of his steed, he struggled to push out thoughts of his family, the time he missed while in the war, and all the broken promises of his teachers. The time had come in which the last straw was broken, and his masters had the gall to break yet another promise.

Upon entering the large stone gateway, Aron and Quartose were met by Epsor and surrounded by a squad of their fellow knights. Quartose furrowed his brow as he looked at the hardened expressions of his comrades. "What is this? What are you doing?"

After a short moment of silence, Epsor raised his long spindly hand. "Quartose, this no longer concerns you." The knights shifted to allow a small opening in their circle for Quartose to pass through before shifting back.

Once free of the encirclement, Quartose marched up to Epsor. "What are you doing? Are you arresting him? You de …"

Epsor quickly cut him off, looking him square in the eyes. "I told you this no longer concerns you. Are you deaf or merely dim-witted?" Then he addressed Aron. "You, Aron, have disobeyed my direct command to return to the academy. We are fighting a war. War is sacrifice, even if that means you cannot be with your family as much as you would like. Such insubordination will not be tolerated. The archris knights are ordered and disciplined, and apparently you lack such qualities. You are hereby under arrest and shall be held in the dungeons until a trial is set."

Aron remained silent as his fellow knights bound his hands with rope. He glowered up at the man he once trusted, Aron's gaze locking with Epsor's. The other hardly reacted at all, neither angry nor saddened by his comrade's arrest. Instead, something else was there, a presence or perhaps an outlook that was deeply hidden within him. "Alright, let's go." The knights, forced Aron forward, leading him down to the small prison cells just below the academy. The academy's holding cells were dark, dank, rusted, and withered. There were only five cells, and only three of them were actually suitable to hold inmates.

The dank prison cell had pools of water on the ground, and little strips of sunlight peeked through the minute cracks in the stone wall. Rats scurried and screeched, endlessly on a mission for food, and large spiders stalked the floor searching for prey. Many of the cell bars were bent and rusted; some even eroded to the point of nonexistence. Yet, it served its purpose and maintained Aron within its disgusting confines. Aron sat upon a relatively small rock in the corner, watching the archris knights pace back and forth on guard duty. His mind swirled, pondering on what had just transpired. *What is Epsor up to? Why did he do this? How can the other archris knights stand for this? I had doubts about coming with Quartose in the first place, and now who knows when I will see my family again?* Aron thought. Clenching his fists, Aron rested his forehead on his knuckles. His pulse quickened, and after a few seconds, he leapt up and kicked the wall over and over again. His right foot became sore, possibly bruised, but Aron did not care. When he at last settled down a bit, he could not sit still. Pacing back and forth in his tiny cell like a trapped wild animal, a thousand images rushed into his mind: some of his wife weeping, others of his daughter. Sadness and anger flooded him. *How could Epsor do this? Epsor is after something, but what?*

The knight's eyes surveyed the cell; he clenched his fists and smiled thinly. Backing up against the wall,

Aron ran forward, shouldering the cell door. His right shoulder throbbed slightly, but hope was rekindled. Aron repeated the process. The locking mechanism groaned in protest. His blood felt like liquid fire in his veins. His pulse quickening, Aron rushed at the door a third time. Clang! The door burst open. After regaining his balance, Aron limped along, his foot scolding him for overexerting himself. Just then, Aron heard movement in the prison. Someone was coming. Bracing himself, he waited anxiously. Perhaps some answers were about to reveal themselves soon. The footsteps abruptly stopped, followed by a loud smack.

"Aron?" a familiar voice called out.

"Quartose? What are you …"

"Your family is in danger. We gotta move now!"

Aron's brow furrowed as he quickly grabbed his friend's arm with more force than he intended. Aron's voice sharpened. "If it concerns my family, we will make time. Now what is going on?"

Releasing a prolonged sigh, Quartose pushed Aron's hand off his shoulder. "There have been reports that a thworf host is carving its way straight for your village."

"What? What does that mean? What could possibly be so valuable to Zontose in Fair Wood?" Aron screamed. Even as the words were breathed out of his mouth, his heart thumped harder; there was only one person in Fair Wood that held any particular significance. "Jori," Aron whispered as his eyes widened.

"What did you say?"

"Nothing," Aron interjected. "Let's get out of here."

Death was nothing foreign to Aron. Being acquainted with battle and death was the nature of being an Archris Knight, but never before had his eyes graced such a sight. Smoke billowed from his home village, and body parts lay strewn about, demonstrating the pleasure the thworfs took in killing. Many were gnawed on and barely recognizable as human, and an overpowering stench of death choked out the smells of nature. As his horse brought him into view of Fair Wood, Aron's mind became cloudy, and his heart beat faster. No emotion could be felt while the shock and terror sank in.

"Ya!" Aron spurred his horse forward, straight into the heart of the ruined city.

"Aron, wait!" Quartose called out, but it was too late.

Aron's horse halted abruptly in front of his home. Leaping down from the saddle, Aron wasted no time running into his ransacked house. As he looked around, his eyes rested upon the one thing he prayed to never see. Tears welled up in the man's eyes, quickly turning to wailing sobs. Before him lay the dismembered corpse of his wife and a little girl. Blood was everywhere. Nina had been torn to shreds, and the little girl was desecrated beyond recognition. His mind reeled with the crushing weight of utter grief. Aron dared not trust his eyes, he could not, and he had to believe this was an illusion. But it wasn't an illusion. Reality was crueler than any nightmare. The war had at last hit home with him, and it had robbed him of his precious family. After what seemed an eternity, he heard his friend's footsteps enter the house.

"May Voshnore have mercy!" Quartose fell to his knees beside his friend, tears welling in his eyes. He could not fathom the pain Aron was enduring. His mind was reeling from his surroundings. Not knowing what to say, he remained silent.

After a moment, Aron slowly rose. "Help me bury them?" he asked solemnly. Quartose silently agreed. Once the process was completed, Aron knelt down at the fresh graves and wept again, tears flowing freely from his eyes, down his stubbly cheeks, onto the soil below.

"Aron, I'm so, so very sorry. If I would have known …"

Another lingering silence endured after Quartose trailed off. At last Aron looked up at his friend. "It was nothing you did." The tears had lightened up. "Zontose is more cunning than we ever realized."

"Zontose? You think *he's* behind this?"

"Are you blind? Look around you! You said yourself Epsor has been acting peculiar, and what you told me in the cell lines up, too." Aron voiced this more to himself than to Quartose. "I don't know what is going on," Aron murmured, tears once again streaming down his cheeks.

# Chapter 3

Two aged spires rose from the ground. The stone that used to be perfect and brilliant white now was yellowed, cracked, and even crumbling in certain areas. Ten acres of grass and flowers wreathed the buildings which were otherwise enclosed by forest. The wind noisily whipped along the field, stroking the banners on the roofs of the two towers, caressing the cotton that was embroidered with the shield of the wizard order. The aroma of spring embraced the wizard's seat of power, something its inhabitants rarely took note of, but it hardly escaped Zan. The tall wizard's white beard flailed as the wind combed through it. Zan clutched his blue cloak close as his booted feet propelled him up the stairs to the West Tower's entrance. His feet slammed against the cracked, tan, stone steps as he ascended upwards. On one particular landing about mid-way to his destination, Zan's eyes caught a new painting, or at least one that had been recently moved. Zan's dark brown eyes scanned the piece of art as he drew near to it, but he was careful not to actually place his fingers upon the pigment.

The piece depicted a battle fought long ago when the wizards were more numerous and worlox demons dominated all of Goandria. In the very center, Lorkai posed, his brilliant wizard's sword flashing green lightning as he vanquished his foes and led the wizards to victory. Alas, that was a different time. After a few minutes of gazing at the immortalized battle scene, Zan shook his head. "What a shame." He continued up the stairs.

Abruptly, the stone steps beneath Zan's feet trembled. The walls shook, causing thin cracks to form in the stone. Bracing himself against the wall, Zan attempted to ascend the stairway to the nearest landing but was thrown back downward. Searing pain shot through the back of his head when his fall came to a halt. Holding his eyes shut and clasping the back of his head, he slowly returned to a standing position. Grasping the window ledge firmly in front of him, Zan peered outside through an onslaught of sudden dizziness. Outside the temples he saw blue flame hovering over the grassy fields, but the flames did not burn the vegetation or rise up from the ground. Curiosity overrode pain as Zan's head craned upward, seeing that the mysterious flames were shooting down from the sky.

Within seconds, an army of wizards flew outside. At least a hundred wizards came to meet their new enemy. They threw lightning, freezing spells, and all matter of wizardry they could at the fiery creature. One wave of fire spiraled downward, sweeping across the front ranks of the wizards, vaporizing nearly one quarter of the army. More wizards poured out, launching an array of attacks at their enemy, but in spite of their persistence, nothing stopped the attacker. The swirling firestorm sped up, turning into a tornado of blue fire that coalesced into a spectral wolf-like form. The creature's final form stood half the size of temples, dwarfing the wizards below. Deep black, glass-like eyes surveyed the scene below as the specter unleashed an unrelenting inferno. Dozens of wizards screamed in agony as the flames devoured them. Blasts of yellow, blue, and green lightning continued raining down upon the spectral foe, but this merely angered it. The area around the temples was now scorched, and hundreds of wizards' bones lay scattered about, and the air began to darken from all the ash floating to the sky.

Zan's knees slowly raised him upright. Cradling his head, he attempted to master the stairs once again. The stench of burnt flesh permeating his nostrils. Zan covered his mouth and nose with his hand, but that did little to stop him from smelling the horrible smell. Again he collapsed on the stairs. His heart thumped wildly, and his eyes grew red and misty. "Why?" He looked up. "Why is this happening to us? So many wizards dead …" Each scream Zan heard was like a knife jabbing into his heart. "I can't give in; not now. There is still time," he mumbled and stumbled back to his feet.

When at last Zan made it to the conference room, he saw the heads of the order gathered around the central ebony table discussing the situation outside. Zan soon realized that calling it a discussion was grossly inaccurate. The wizard council members were hurling insults and bickering like a group of children trying to decide who was going to play with a new toy. Zan cleared his throat, hoping to get the council's attention, but he was ignored or not heard. White hot anger flashed through him, and Zan slammed his sword down onto the table. "Are we seriously going to bicker amongst ourselves while we are under attack?" Zan's voice abruptly cut in.

"Zan? We were wondering if you would ever come," one of the wizards commented pleasantly.

"You look terrible. What happened?" another asked.

Zan shook his head in disbelief, eyeing each one of the wizards seated around the table. "Our people are dying painfully, and you are sitting here arguing?"

"We do not know what to do. Nothing we use does anything!" a wizard blurted defensively.

"And that justifies your behavior? Shame on you; shame on you all!"

The wizard council sat quietly, waiting for someone to speak first, but no one did.

"What do you suggest, Zan?" someone finally spoke up.

"Well, I think a great starting point is understanding our enemy. That thing outside wields powers similar to ours. How is that possible?" Zan said.

"There is only one who has ever managed to twist our powers," a tall, blonde woman draped in a cloak said.

"That abomination destroyed himself," another swiftly cut in.

"What if the prophecy is true?"

"Of course the prophecy is true. It came from Voshnore himself."

"There is no proof of that!"

"Harkendor is dead."

The wizards erupted again. "Enough!" Zan blurted out. "Is this really what you want to discuss while our people are being slaughtered outside? Can't you see we are under attack? You all seek any opportunity to insult and argue with one another, don't you?"

The building shook violently again, causing hairline cracks to appear in the stone. Silence abruptly fell on the wizards. Wide-eyed glances were exchanged across the table, and Zan's eyes abruptly shifted to the nearby window. A searing blue flash was followed by shrieks of hundreds suddenly perishing outside. Another rumble vibrated the building, and the conference room exploded with energy. Zan shielded his eyes from the blast as some of the stone collapsed. When he removed his arm from his face, a great dust cloud lingered in the room. A hole had been blasted in the wall from the outside. Blood was everywhere.

"What just happened, Sonja?"

"Our power, it … it …"

"Quick! We must protect ourselves!" Zan said.

"How? At the rate in which …"

"Just do it!" Zan cut in.

A single ebony eye peered through the hole in the structure, staring straight at Zan. The wizard froze. The deep black eye, enveloped in blue flame, studied him for an instant, and then a fury of blue fire entered the remains of the conference chamber. The firestorm illuminated the room then transformed into a humanoid form. The being's black eyes silently surveyed the room, looking at the crushed wizards under the rubble, finally resting upon Sonja. "Ah, how the mighty wizards have fallen! So weak and pathetic," a deep, thundering voice jeered.

"What … who?" Sonja gasped, staring straight into the black eyes, frozen in fear.

The being laughed malevolently. "I am the one who has come to reclaim his prize for ridding this world of the worlox," the creature announced as he wrapped his fingers around the woman's neck and slowly raised her. Her unblinking eyes stared straight into the monster before her body burst into flames. "No!" Zan shouted.

"The last of the ruling wizards. Come. Defend yourself! Oh, but you can't! The powers your order has hoarded to themselves are quickly fading. You can feel it, can't you?"

"We will stop you!"

Deep laughter rumbled from the creature again. "How? You will die with the rest unless you surrender yourselves and pledge your loyalty to me."

"We would never."

"I imagined that would be the case. Everyone in Goandria will burn and suffer my wrath, and there is nothing you can do about it! Goandria is sick and dying. I have come to remove the infected flesh and restore this world."

"No!" Zan screamed, unleashing a torrent of wizard lightning.

The demon absorbed the blast with ease. "Now, now. Don't be so foolish."

"Who are you?" Zan demanded.

"I am the one who brings darkness to the wizards, the one who brought order to Goandria long ago. I have returned."

Staggering backward, Zan's eyes widened. "Harkendor," he breathed. "It can't be, it just can't be. You destroyed yourself."

"Not everything is as it seems, dear wizard."

"You won't win. We will survive, and when we resurface, your reign will be at an end. You will be defeated. Voshnore will protect Goandria."

"Such an idealistic fool. Where is your god now? Why doesn't Voshnore come to save you while your temples burn and your people die? All of Goandria will realize the truth as I once did. The path to victory stands apart from Voshnore, because it is in our hands to protect our world, not his. I am the god of Goandria now."

With his last bit of strength, Zan reached out his hand, palm facing forward, and released a bright white energy field. The energy filled the room with a piercing white light and expanded rapidly. Other wizards noticed and used what remained of their power to aid the process.

Inside the conference room, Harkendor groaned. His face contorted as he attempted to protect himself from the light. "You can't stop me!" The dark wizard shrieked as the energy intensified. His flames diminished, and his essence shrank. The once black eyes now appeared gray as he writhed in agony.

"I already have." With an explosion of energy, the fire essence of Harkendor was dispelled. The atmosphere felt pure again, the dampening evil presence was gone, and reality at last had a chance to sink in. The remaining wizards gathered outside and observed the opaque dome of mystical energy that now encompassed the blessed temples. The wizards were protected but powerless. Zan knew the war would have to continue without them.

A single horse drew a rusted vehicle down the winding, gravel road. The black coat of the animal glistened in the setting sunlight as the eastern wind combed through its mane. Powerful muscles flexed, propelling the beast and the carriage behind it. A small dab of blood began to stain the ebony hair of the steed after its master's whip cracked yet again. Upon the driver's seat of the carriage, if a carriage it could be called, sat a particularly large thworf. His one good eye glistened as it focused on the dismayed steed. Black lips curled, revealing sharp, rotting teeth.

The steel box on wheels creaked and moaned every time it encountered a bump or dip in the road. Oxidization covered every inch of the carriage, eating small portholes that allowed the lone passenger to get small glimpses outside. The girl inside huddled against the back, unable to stand or sit upright due to the cramped conditions of the carriage.

The creatures flanking the carriage did not make a sound, their weapons ever at the ready, and their powerful, stocky bodies clad in chainmail. A mighty black dragon flew above, its fierce rider keeping his luminescent blue eyes on the soldiers below. All around the army of thworfs was a blanket of cold. As the army marched onward, trees and plants froze or withered and died, animals hurried away, and no bird or insect could be heard. The rancid odor of death and decay was replete along the road, the smell intensifying as they marched along, becoming too much for even the thworfs, but they all knew better than to complain.

The black dragon abruptly swooped to the front of the lines, planting its talons firmly on the gravel road as it reared up and unleashed a mini-volcano into the sky. The rider hopped off his saddle. Heavy leather boots thudded on the ground, and glowing blue eyes surveyed his troops, looking upon each individual simultaneously. Every thworf stood incredibly still, careful to not gaze directly at the dark one. The shadow-figure's black cloak billowed in the breeze, revealing the long, gray tunic and cruel weapon dangling at its belt. "We make camp here for the night. Has the prisoner been fed?" The voice sounded like a scratchy-hiss emanating from behind the black hood.

The thworf captain stepped forward, careful to look past or through his leader instead of at it. "No, sir. We've been marching for four days straight. Not even the men have been able to eat."

A low hiss rumbled from the dark creature as its eyes bore into the thworf. Without warning, it swiftly drew its sword and beheaded the captain. "Zontose said to bring the girl to him swiftly and unharmed." Several foot soldiers scrabbled for the last of their rations and opened up the carriage. The food was hurriedly tossed inside before the hinges creaked closed again.

The din of thworfs setting up camp echoed through the small carriage. The girl wrapped herself with a tattered cloak that once was her mother's. Her face stayed covered until she was absolutely certain the nasty creatures wouldn't be disturbing her. She then viciously grabbed the food, devouring the bland rations. Sniffles made their way out between mouthfuls of food. The girl's cheeks were soaked, and her eyes were crimson and puffy. Once she finished her food, she curled back up in her corner and closed her eyes. She thumbed the fabric on the cloak. Dirt was caked within its fibers. Her nails dug into it over and over as tears began to well up in her eyes once more. Her mind continually replayed the horror she endured just before her capture, the look in her mother's eyes as she died. Her eyes went upward. "Oh, Voshnore, please help me," she whispered softly.

Days went by, countless days. The girl was sustained by old bread and salted meat. Finally the carriage came to a halt and the creaky hinge whined open again. A clawed, gray hand reached in and yanked her outside. The young girl's eyes widened, for she saw neither plains nor forests. Instead she saw a barren landscape layered in rust-colored soil. Not a plant, tree, or body of water could be seen. All around, plateaus and distant mountains rose up, covered in the same cracked, red soil as the ground beneath her feet. The arid wind whipped without hindrance, flinging grains of sand with it. An odd, musty aroma filled her nostrils, but no source of moisture could be found. Thousands upon thousands of thworf units stood at the ready, and many more were attending to massive furnaces, fueling the fires, and hammering out weapons. Other thworf units oversaw the continual flow of supply wagons; the carts were wide enough for four humans to lie side by side in the bed and could carry loads up to six-feet high. A hand abruptly whirled her around and shoved her onward.

A black stone tower spiraled high above the cloud cover. Torchlight flickered in the windows and several banners bearing a symbol the girl did not recognize waved in the wind on either side of the entrance. The squad of thworfs yanked the chain around her neck periodically to ensure the young girl kept pace as she marched through a sea of thworfs toward the fortress' entrance. As she came closer to the gates, the musty odor diminished, and instead she smelled sweat and body soil. She felt the eyes of the thworf army upon her as they made way for her to pass. A brief moment of curiosity caused the girl to stare at the thousands of soldiers waiting at attention. No one gave orders, and no one spoke. There was only silence and stillness across the thworf masses.

Massive ebony gates marked the entrance to the tower. The stone gates groaned open, and out marched four beings heavily armored from head to toe in dark steel. In the middle was a black cloaked figure with a brown leather jerkin covering his torso. His gaze quickly shifted to the girl. The girl's pulse quickened and her face contorted at the sight of the creature's familiar luminous blue eyes. Behind the hood of this dark creature was a vague image of a ghastly yellow skull. No gloves graced the ghastly, skeletal hands protruding from its sleeves. The thworfs brought her forward, inclining their heads slightly as the creature emerged from the tower. The other creature dismounted from his black dragon, making his way toward the one at the gate.

"She is the one the master requested," the shadow creature hissed to the other.

A wet gurgling sound, slightly resembling an inhale of oxygen, emanated from the other. Then he turned to the army before him. "The master has obtained his prize!" A thunderous roar came from the thworf legions. "Through his might, we will conquer the Three Republics and Goandria! None can oppose us! Lord Zontose's will shall be the driving force of the expansion of our great empire. You are the fists of that will. Go forth and make war on those who resist his plans." Another roar of jubilation boomed through the barren terrain. Simultaneously, the thworf masses turned, and their heavy boots stomped in unison as they funneled from their land to the Three Republics. War chants sounded as they moved. The girl's jaw hung open at the terrible sight before her, tears once again streaming down her cheeks, but she made no sound.

The beast from the fortress turned to face the girl. "Welcome to Morhelgol, tower of the mighty Zontose. This is your home now, Jori, and you *will* serve him." The girl said nothing as the creature and his guards led her through the massive tower. Inside, the walls were constructed of shiny black stone, though some of the rooms they went past were decorated with red oak. The icy presence of the shadow creature caused the condensation on the stone walls to immediately turn to frost, which melted again after he passed. Jori shivered uncontrollably, and her breath was visible in spite of the relative warmth of Morhelgol. Torch light danced dimly in the tower. The glowing blue eyes of the other shadow creature became more visible the deeper inside they went. Unlike a human's eyes that would dart around to take in sights, the creature's blue orbs remained ever in one position.

The girl was led up a staircase, down a hall, and up another set of stairs. This pattern continued about four times until at last the creature motioned for the guards to halt. The creature stopped before a large entry blocked by oak double doors, its ghastly hands hastily turned the nobs, and the doors flung open. Jori gingerly walked into the room. Beautiful paintings of distant lands accented the walls, a large bed with blue silk sheets sat in the corner, and a stained glass window, which appeared out of place, on the eastern wall depicted a rising sun over a wilderness landscape. Wooden toys were piled high in an open chest: horses, soldiers, baby dolls, and other various forms to encourage a child's imagination. Jori surveyed the room, slowly walking further in. After, looking around with an unreadable expression, she ran into the corner and began to sob again. The creature's hypnotic eyes rested on Jori. Only once did she return the gaze, and in that moment, she felt the weight of his stare. Her heart pounded, and she froze; the source of the rivers flowing down her cheeks stopped producing fluids temporarily while the young girl stared into the grotesque figure before her. The lingering presence of the shadow creature brought a blanket of cold in the room. Frost emerged on the walls then swiftly turned to thin ice buildup.

Suddenly the creature turned and waved to the guards to follow. The door slammed shut behind them, and a heavy lock clanged into place. Jori gasped and sprinted for the door, fingering the knob and violently jerking on it, confirming her worst fears. "Hey! Hey! Let me out!" she screamed, beating her fists on the door until they became reddened and bruised. She eventually gave up, crumpled to the floor, and cradled her face in the palms of her hands. Tears resumed their flow from her eyes.

The creature's luminous blue eyes were the only things visible in the unlit corridors. Ice spread more rapidly than usual around the shadow figure as it moved along. At last it came to a massive doorway lit by a single torch and guarded by two thworf sentries. The creature paid no heed to the thworfs and pushed its way through the stone doors. Inside the chamber, hundreds of torches burst to life and the doors slammed shut behind the beast. The room, in spite of its size, was a rather plain, simple, stone room with a mezzanine above. A hooded figure moved along the cracked stone stairs. The creature immediately bowed. "Master," it said in a low tone.

"You and your kind's powers are growing, friend. I take it you were successful in finding the girl?" the hooded one asked.

"Yes, she is here now."

"Excellent. I am troubled, though, about something. I ordered you and your kind to find her and bring her here, not to get involved directly. The thworfs were supposed to sack Fair Wood and find her without you. Were my instructions unclear?" the hooded man questioned.

"N n-no master. The thworfs are fools. I did not want …"

The other swiftly raised his hand, cutting off the creature. "You were not to reveal yourselves too early!" the man's voice thundered. "If anyone knows you and your brothers have returned, I will be exposed too early."

"For-for-give me m-my l-lord."

The man walked closer to his servant and pulled back his hood, resting a middle-aged hand upon the creature. "You have done well in bringing me the girl, Daest. However, if word spreads that the osodars have returned, I will no longer be able to remain in the shadows."

Then blue-green fire erupted from the hooded man's hands, enveloping the osodar. The creature thrashed around wildly on the floor, kicking incessantly as its robes disintegrated to ash. An inhuman scream emanated from the creature. The flames reflected off the hooded man's dark eyes as he watched the tormented being squirm in agony. When the flames died and the osodar's robes were no more, the creature crawled back to his master's feet. The osodar's true visage was revealed: an immaterial, transparent, skeletal being with a yellow and green hue encompassing its being.

"I … I … I will not fail you again." The osodar's voice quavered.

"No, you won't," the hooded man said coolly. "Now gather the other osodars and inform them they are not to leave Dalarashess until instructed."

A cloud of dust swirled behind the two horses as their hooves clacked along the road. Rows of evergreens lined the path that carved its way through the woods, and birds called to one another, composing music of a gentle nature. The sun beat down relentlessly, unhindered by clouds, glistening upon bright red wildflowers that dotted the surrounding woodland. Quartose's blue eyes studied his friend riding on the other horse. Aron sat utterly silent. After some time, Quartose turned his gaze away, staring down the long, narrow, winding road before them. His thoughts wandered to the hundreds of times he traveled this road. It was the only path that connected the heart of the Republics and the outlying rural areas. Memories flashed of a time before the war with Zontose, when travelers were common and bandits were the scariest part of the journey. For over two weeks, the knights carried on down the road, never encountering traveler or robber.

Hours turned into days, and the silence loomed. Quartose's mind sifted through conversation starters, but Aron's unflinching, distant stare made him rethink the wisdom in talking at all. As the days trailed on, Quartose often shifted uncomfortably after spending so long on the back of a warhorse. At night the two travelers would stop and make camp. Neither had any food to eat, but sometimes the land would yield a few handfuls of wild berries. Aron ate very little, even when the opportunity came, and Quartose only occasionally saw his friend take a drink from his water skin. Aron's long, matted, dirty hair hid most of his face. His head rarely turned, and the fingers on his left hand were ever running across his chin and upper lip.

This routine carried on for nearly a month, all the while Aron remained silent and closed off. At first Quartose hoped it was a temporary byproduct of grief, but as the weeks passed and not so much as a grunt was spoken, he found it difficult to think of anything else. The beautiful woodland all around them, something of which Quartose often took notice, no longer held value. He began to lose his appetite and continually found his eyes fixed upon Aron, secretly wishing the circumstances would change. *Perhaps I should say something? Perhaps the grief is still too fresh? What if he suddenly took a vow of silence after the loss of his family?* These questions swirled around in his mind over and over again. Just then, something caught Quartose's ear, and he saw four figures charging toward them: mounted archris knights.

The oncoming riders abruptly halted at the sight of their comrades. One, who had silver hair and a long beard to match, spoke up first. "Aron, Quartose? You were the last people I expected to see."

"The knighthood has fallen into disarray since your escape. Many say Epsor has gone mad. After you broke out, he personally executed those who were standing guard, causing the knights at the academy to revolt."

"What?! Epsor doesn't have the authority to carry out executions!" Aron exclaimed.

Whirling his head around, Quartose's jaw dropped and eyes widened. Aron's gaze met his friend's, and he quickly smiled thinly.

"Epsor has been branded a traitor and has since disappeared. No one saw him flee; it was like he vanished into thin air. Rumor has it that he is in league with Zontose and that's how the thworfs are managing attacks so far into the Republics," the older knight said.

"Attacks?" Quartose said, glancing at Aron.

"You don't know? Ilva is under attack. The city was ordered to evacuate. We were sent to look for reinforcements. Isn't that where you are headed?" the silver-haired knight said.

"Well yes, but not for that reason. My village, Fair Wood, was razed. We are on our way to the archris fortress in the city to warn them," Aron said.

"The fortress is completely destroyed," one of the four riders said.

"I didn't expect to find two knights so conveniently close to the action," the silver-haired man said.

"We will do what we can, but our presence will hardly turn the tide," Aron said.

"No, but it's a start. We are hoping more will join us from the Grivear Academy," another rider said.

"Good luck. From what you said, it sounds like you are going to need it," Aron said.

"Indeed. Well, we best be off now. Thank you for your help." The older knight spurred his horse, the other riders trailing behind.

Once they were gone, Quartose threw up his hands, shaking his head at Aron. "I've been worried sick about you! I thought you were having some sort of mental break-down or something, and all of a sudden you break your silence and depression for a few strangers?"

"I'm sorry."

"You don't need to be sorry. I get it. You endured a painful loss, but I just needed to know you were okay."

"I really wasn't, though, and I'm still not." Tears began to run down his reddened cheeks. "I'm constantly reminded of them. I have nothing to live for anymore, nothing except bringing down the monster that did this. Come, the battlefield awaits us!" Before Quartose could respond, Aron sent his horse barreling down the road to Ilva.

# Chapter 4

As the months passed, thousands more thworfs poured into the Three Republics. Village after village was razed to the ground, causing a surge of refugees to flood into the major cities. Every archris knight and local soldier was called to arms. Every day more lost their lives and more legions of thworfs marched on the Republics. Hordes of black dragons scorched the land; fires were everywhere, raining ash down upon the cities. The armies of the Three Republics eventually abandoned the outlying settlements, redirecting their efforts to protect the major cities. After eight months, only three cities—Grivear City, Belthora, and Hondor—stood between the thworf army and the utter collapse of the Three Republics.

Grivear City quickly scrambled to defend itself from the onslaught of thworf hordes. Tens of thousands of thworfs and dragons marched to the grand capital of the Republics. Amethyst colored dragons were at the head of the charge. These larger dragons bore sharp, poisoned spines from head to tail. Their blue fire scorched through the polished white stone walls that protected the city. Massive siege ladders slapped against the walls, and thworfs hurriedly crawled into Grivear City. The siege lasted three months until at last the defenses collapsed. The remaining people retreated to Hondor of Ashear, the new capital of the republics, and Belthora, the governing seat of Verntail.

One travel-worthy road remained within the razed capital. A young man, probably in his late teens, clad in soot-covered clothes that nearly qualified as rags, cunningly darted through the ruins. His target was at last in sight. Just a few hundred more feet and he would be there. Kneeling beside a brick slab that once was a wall, his eyes scanned the area several times before he moved on. All around, the voices of thworfs and the clatter of metal armor could be heard. The coast was clear. Dashing onward once more, he took cover again to check his surroundings. He then ran the rest of the way to his objective: a lonely, brown horse tied to a railing. He prayed the steeds of Zontose's army were not as ill-tempered as the soldiers as he quickly unstrapped the horse. Half surprised the horse didn't buck and run away its first chance, the young man wasted no time hopping on its back. His chance for escape had come at last.

Galloping down the dusty roadway was far more difficult than he had anticipated. Debris and bodies were everywhere, the smoke and fires made seeing where he was going nearly impossible, and an overwhelming darkness pressed upon him. The stench of death permeated his very soul. The multitude that once dwelt here covered the ground as grass does a hillside. To make matters worse, thworf patrols littered the remains of the city. Why so many were left behind to guard a ruined city was beyond him. Often the young horseman halted his advance to duck past unfriendly eyes. Grivear was the largest city in the Republics, sprawling to a radius of ten miles with massive walls enclosing it. The sheer size of the ruins, coupled with the setting sun, made him question the wisdom of his attempted escape.

The rider looked up and saw the last remnant of sunlight plunge below the western horizon. In the infancy of night, howls, moans and other clamor echoed, accompanied by scores of eyes emerging from the darkest places. For the first time in the youth's life, he prayed they were just thworfs and not something worse in the service of Zontose.

Overhead, a squadron of black dragons circled before the full moon light. Spurring his horse even harder, the rider and steed hastily navigated through the city ruins. Mounted upon two of the dragons which flew lower than the rest, dark figures scanned the surface for their prey. The air became icy rather quickly, so fast that frost formed on the back of the rider's hands in just a few minutes. Suddenly, a black dragon bellowed, and its fellow winged beasts dove after the youth. From behind the charred buildings, thworf squads emerged, running on all fours in attempts to flank the rider. Before him, four massive beings landed so hard the ground cracked and quaked beneath them. The creatures stood ten feet tall, covered almost completely in thick, bronze-plate armor, save for their wings and just enough to reveal their feline appearance. The shape of their bodies revealed an obviously feminine frame, and from behind their bronze helms, green eyes with vertical pupils bore into him. The enemy at last managed to corner him. All four beings simultaneously withdrew dual claymores. One osodar landed his dragon before the young man. The feline beings inclined their heads slightly out of respect then quickly returned their attention to their prey.

"Why do you flee?" the osodar taunted.

Finding himself at a loss for words, the rider remained quiet.

"Is it fear? The master has been searching for you." The dark creature hissed as it drew its own weapon.

The rider kicked the horse's ribs, sending the steed trampling through a half dozen thworfs. The osodars sent the feline creatures in, their clamors bashing aside thworf allies that stood in their way. One simply leapt over the thworf masses and landed on the horse, crushing its skull and catapulting the rider. As his enemies closed in around him, the young man tightly gripped a kitchen knife he had snagged from his torched home.

From atop a building, another warrior pounced on the feline as she attempted to grab the horseman. The warrior's long, dark hair flowed as he rammed his sword through the giant's spine. The crumbling creature crushed several more thworfs as its body fell to the ground. The man withdrew a long dagger and sword and started slashing his way through the thworfs with both weapons. Although vastly outnumbered, the warrior could not be hindered. Thworf after thworf attempted to subdue the newcomer but to no avail. The three remaining felines advanced. Rolling underneath one, the man cut her hamstrings before proceeding to behead another thworf. As the young man watched in shock and awe, he caught a glimmer of the warrior's sword. He was not an ordinary man but an archris knight.

"Get out of here!" the knight screamed. "What are you waiting for? Run!" He cut down a few more foes before he took his own advice. The two of them fled as fast as they could down the rubble-littered roadway. The knight led the young man toward a large building with a small gap at the bottom. "Get in!" the knight barked.

"But I can't fit in there …"

"Get in or die. It's that simple, friend."

Sighing, the youth wormed his way through the hole, groaning the entire time. The knight quickly followed suit and gathered stones and other rubble to pile in front of the entry.

"Where did you come from?"

"We need to keep moving. That won't hold them for long," the knight answered.

"Can I at least get your name? And where exactly do you propose we move to? We are blockaded inside a building."

"The name's Aron. I've already scouted this area. This building looks like it goes further underground. Maybe it connects with the underground network that was built under the city long ago."

"Maybe? You brought us in here based on a maybe?"

"Do you always complain this much, kid?" Aron sighed.

"I have a name, too. It's Mathil, not kid. What are you doing here?"

"You ask a lot of questions."

"Uh, well, considering the circumstances …"

"The king sent me to look for survivors. Come on; we don't have time," Aron cut him off. "Help me look for something we can make into torches."

"I don't really see anything worth using," said Mathil.

"That could make things difficult." The clamor of their foes was now right outside the building. "We are just going to have to navigate the best we can."

Excessively jagged stones lined the bottom of the tunnels through which the two men traversed. The rocks varied greatly in size; some were mere pebbles while others were about six inches in diameter. The soles of their boots quickly became shredded, and the other portions of the footwear were torn and scuffed. Many of the troublesome stones pierced their feet as they walked. What remained of their boots became sticky, and their gait quickly digressed to limping. Only the faintest of light illuminated the passage before them. Minute minerals in the stone that lined the tunnels gave off an iridescent crimson glow. It was hardly enough to see where they were going; Aron could barely make out the stone wall inches to his left. The walls were no less sharp than the ground, so their hands had become bloodied and skinned as they navigated purely by touch. Eventually the underground passage began to incline, slightly at first, but the slope steepened. After about a half hour of climbing, the passage abruptly leveled off, and then they came to a fork.

Mathil stopped. His eyes widened and looked to Aron, but the knight continued left as if he didn't even notice the intersection. "This is some escape plan, Aron. After who knows how long down here, we still don't know how to get out!" Mathil suddenly exclaimed, shattering Aron's thoughts. "Aren't you in the least bit concerned we might be trapped down here? At least up at the surface we would have died fighting."

"We aren't lost," Aron said.

"Really? And how do you figure that? If you know where we are going, why didn't you give some sort of indication when we came to an intersection?"

"You are following me, are you not?"

"I guess, if you mean feeling aimlessly along a near-pitch-black tunnel system."

Aron didn't respond. He shook his head slightly and kept moving. Mathil, however wasn't quite done. "See, you just deflected the question. We are lost!"

"Enough! We have about fifty more paces down this stretch, and then we take the next left. Also, in case you have forgotten, if it wasn't for these tunnels we would be dead by now, so show a little gratitude," Aron said.

"I need to rest," Mathil said matter-of-factly.

"We have to keep moving. Who knows if any thworfs are tracking us?"

"Don't you think we would have heard them? They aren't exactly quiet."

Aron chuckled for a moment, then it transformed into full out laughter. Perplexed, Mathil merely stared at the other and wondered if he had gone mad. Once the knight's laughter subsided, Aron took in a deep breath and let it loose slowly. "Well, I suppose you're right. We can spare a few moments and rest."

Mathil curled up on the ground underneath his cloak. It wasn't long before his mind nestled into slumber. Aron lay on his back with hands behind his head, his eyes fixated on the shimmering minerals that glinted all around him. It was in that moment that he realized just how quiet it was down there. A few distant drops of water pinged in the background, but it was a silence unlike anything he had experienced in quite a long time. A thin smile spread across his face. He thought back to all the noisy battles, the annoying crickets, and the storms that made him wish for peace and quiet. Now that he had it, it was too quiet. His mind drifted to the young man beside him. Aron wondered who he was, what brought him to this point, and how he'd managed to be one of the only survivors in a city decimated by thworfs.

Slowly, exhaustion overtook the knight. Glimpses of the life he once had flashed in front him, a life in which he had a family and friends, before the tide of the war shifted in Zontose's favor. His mind's eye saw Jori's sweet smile once again. He could feel her soft cheek once more. He remembered her temper tantrums, how she would throw her toys in a fit of rage because she didn't get her way, and how he wished for a brief period in those moments to be free of her. Now Aron would do anything to see his daughter again, exactly as she was. Aron saw Nina: her beautiful pale skin, her brown hair perfectly draping around her face, accenting its features. Then all turned black. Aron heard his family cry out to him, but he could not reach them. He ran as fast as his body could carry him, but the gap between them would not close.

Aron's eyes snapped open. As his hand reached for a dagger, he screamed so loudly Mathil jumped up, hitting his head on the stone wall behind him. "What! What is going on?" Mathil panted.

Covered in sweat, Aron breathed heavily. He quickly placed the dagger back in its scabbard. "Nothing. It was just a dream."

"A dream? It sounded like you were being murdered! Do you get many like that?"

"I'm not sure."

"Well, it's a wonder we could sleep at all on the stones. My back is killing me. Guess that's what happens when you haven't slept in a while, huh?"

"I, uh, guess. We should get going. We are going to need to find water soon," Aron said.

The two men hastily gathered their things and continued their trek down the rugged tunnels. Once again, Mathil didn't hesitate to voice his complaints about the situation, but Aron simply tuned him out. He kept telling himself that the teenager probably hadn't experienced a hard day's work in his life, but if he were honest, there was a part of him that agreed with Mathil. It had been over ten years since Aron had been in the tunnels below Grivear City, and he never remembered them being this miserable. His body groaned with every step, and blood squished out of the holes in his boots. *I feel terrible, my feet are killing me, and this guy next to me won't stop grumbling. When will I wake up from this nightmare?* He thought as he glowered at Mathil.

"Look, a light! Maybe we can get out of here soon," Mathil abruptly exclaimed.

"What is that? It's too small to be torchlight," Aron said.

"Come on. Let's check it out!" Mathil said, excitedly running off.

"Mathil, wait!" Aron called out, chasing after the boy.

As they ran, more and more lights popped up amidst the darkness. A sea of deep blue eyes suddenly lit up and stared unflinchingly at the strangers. Over fifty sets of eyes bore into the two men. The eyes of the beings were the deepest blue either of the two men had seen in the entirety of their lives. They were like oblong sapphires resting in the palest of faces. The large eyes reminded Aron of the osodars' but in a way that completely contrasted them. Where the osodars' gaze brought terror, there was a peace about these other creatures, an innocence their demeanor gave off. The mass of beings were very diminutive by human standards, standing roughly a foot tall, with pale skin so white that it reflected the light of their miniature torches. The creatures' hair was all uniformly the same color as their skin, about shoulder length, and so glossy it looked like strands of soft metal growing from their scalps.

"Oh, thank the Heavens! Voshnore brings us more survivors!" said one of the small beings.

Before either man could get in a word, another pale creature stepped forward. "Ah, yes, yes! They are weary. We shall bring them back with the others."

"Do you know what these things are?" Mathil blurted.

"Only by legends. I didn't think they existed, but I read about them in the histories. They are ferrorians. If the legends are true, basically, what you see is what you get. They have been largely inactive in history, or ignored perhaps."

"Come, come, we take you to our city. There you will be safe." Another ferrorian beamed, taking Aron by his little finger and leading the way.

# Chapter 5

Dozens of torches reflected off the polished, black, stone walls. A massive picture window allowed the light of the full moon to give the room an eerie glow. On the adjacent wall, the giant stained-glass window depicted one of the wizard battles of old. Within the room was a lone figure, encased in dark armor and hooded in a green cloak. The man hunched over several large books spread across an oak desk.

Abruptly, the doors to his chamber swung open, and an osodar stepped forward and patiently knelt before the man. "You wish to see me, master?"

The hooded figure did not respond. He continued poring over his books, running his index finger along certain sections, and mumbling to himself. After several minutes had passed, the hooded man turned to the osodar. "Daest, this war is winding down to a close. I can feel it. The corruption and oppression of the Three Republics is nearly at an end. You and the others must see to it that total victory is ours. Crush what remains of the republics. However, victory will not come entirely by force. The people must be shown a new way, a way of order and peace. You will be the instrument of order, and our guest will prove vital to restoring peace. Your brutality has impacted that potential and left me … *displeased.*"

A slight tremor traveled down the other's back. "My lord, you told me to get her to talk. She hasn't. She barely eats, she …"

"I didn't ask for excuses. I think it's time I introduced myself to the seer. You are my greatest servant, Daest. If we are to rule, your cruelty must cease. Now, prepare the army for the final invasion of the Three

Republics. Do what you must to accomplish the task, but now is not the time for the brutality of old. If you forget that, there will be consequences."

"As you wish, lord, but it's been a year, and you have said nothing about these tactics. I merely thought I was doing your will."

A thin smile creased the face of the hooded man. "Indeed." The hooded man followed the osodar out of the room, the large, black, stone doors slamming on their own behind him. Strolling down the long, dark corridors, he made his way to a room on the level below. Before entering, the hooded man's cloak and black armor transformed into a simple gray tunic and leggings. His now dirt-smudged hand slowly turned the doorknob, and the massive wooden slab swung open. Inside, Jori sat with her knees pressed against her chest at the foot of the bed. She was covered in dirt and bruises. Blood stains dotted her clothes, and her hair was matted into knots.

"My dear, are you all right?" he asked gently.

Jori simply looked at him silently.

The man slowly walked over to the girl and knelt down. "It's okay. You can trust me. The monsters don't know I'm here."

"Who are you?"

"Oh, I'm just a servant. I was captured years ago by those vile creatures."

Jori continued to eye the other, then after a moment turned and stared at the wall in the other direction.

The hooded man's brow furrowed slightly, then he spoke up again. "Oh, my child, what have they done to you?" Gently taking Jori's arm, the man examined the cuts and bruises that lined it. Jori said nothing in response and continued staring off at the wall.

"Look, I know you just met me, but I'm a friend. I can help you."

"There are no friends here," said Jori.

The hooded man hovered his hands over her arm. The wounds instantly disappeared. "See, I told you I am a friend." He smiled.

Torrential rain hammered against the black stone of Morhelgol. Lightning flashed nearby, threatening to strike the mighty tower. In the highest room of the fortress, Zontose sat alone. A tankard of ale resting upon the wide throne armrest reflected a brief flash of lightning, illuminating the man's dark face. His right thumb rubbed over the tankard's handle, which was shaped like a dragon, as he unflinchingly gazed out the window before him. Outside, thousands of his servants bustled, each one attempting to accomplish a specific task in spite of the weather. Thworfs were working the forges. More katzians had arrived from their own land to serve Zontose in further perfecting the army's training and seeking to find the ideal soldiers.

Suddenly something caught his eye. Far below, Zontose saw two figures arguing, followed by blades being drawn and a fight breaking out. He released a sigh and rapped his left fingers on the armrest. His eyes were quickly distracted, but his mind could not help but linger on the situation. His darkened eyes peered below. More fighting had erupted. This time a score of thworfs were at each others' throats. *I will leave it to the general*, Zontose thought to himself, but he had a nagging feeling that he should see what was happening. Zontose hastily got up from his throne and marched to the belly of the fortress.

After nearly thirty minutes, he was at Morhelgol's gates. The massive doors swung themselves open with tremendous force; the echo of the metal immediately silenced everyone.

"What is the meaning of this?" Zontose's voice boomed.

The mob parted, revealing a slightly bruised thworf who was vastly larger than his kin. In his left hand he firmly held a black battle axe, the blade stained with blood. A few feet away, a headless thworf lay. "Forgive me, lord. I attempted to quell the riot, but things quickly got out of hand."

"What is going on here? Or do I need to ask again?"

"No, lord. There are rumors of blasphemes against you germinating in our ranks. This one," the thworf laid his hand on one to the right of him, "attempted to defend the truth, but the traitor you now see dead claimed that we …" The large thworf swallowed hard, looking down at the ground.

"We what?" Zontose urged.

"That we had been duped into being your slaves, Master," the large one stated quickly.

When such talk had previously arisen, Zontose publicly and creatively executed those spreading such ideas. This time, no green lighting or fire erupted from his hands, and no sword was drawn. Zontose's heavy feet clomped forward a few steps, and he levitated himself so that all could see.

A smile cracked Zontose's hardened face, causing some thworfs to flinch. "Friends, I address you as such because that is what you are. You are not my slaves, but my allies. This war has been long and hard. Many more were lost than any of us could have foreseen. I have been harsh with you, not tolerating any failure, but instead asking for your absolute trust and obedience. I understand how some can despair. Our armies are not what they once were, but do you dare turn your backs on our cause now? Do you dare let your oppressors go unpunished when we are at the doorstep of utter victory and total annihilation of the Three Republics? So that we may have order and peace, there can be no room for error in our conquest. Did I not promise that you would rule the new world we built together? Have we not sent our enemies cowering in the corner, dreading our very names?" Zontose's voice deepened with a raspy edge. "Any who oppose this vision oppose you personally and desire for you to be back in the yoke of oppression! We will show the dogmatic people that Voshnore will not hear their cries, that he will not lift a finger to save them, just as he neglected you. I am the new Lord of Goandria, for I have saved its people! I will finish what I started long ago in another time." Zontose's visage began to glow with blue fire. "This war has value beyond individual lives, beyond the wariness you feel. It is the beginning of an era Goandria has never witnessed before!"

An ecstatic applause erupted from the audience below. They shook their swords to the sky, crying out, "Zontose! Zontose!" After several minutes, the master of Dalarashess was met by the large thworf again. "That was brilliant, lord. Just what our people needed."

"Indeed, general, but I am afraid that is not all that was needed. It takes more than a passionate speech to quell dissidence. There is more that needs to be done."

"Name it, and I will see to it personally."

"There is one with great power and great passion, one who could be the key to ultimately reminding all who is the true master."

"But the seer is already in our custody ..." the large thworf began.

"My work with Jori is incomplete and has a significant role to play, but the one I refer to is my queen."

The large thworf's brow furrowed. "Queen, sire?"

Zontose didn't reply. He simply continued on his way.

An old man covered in a black, hooded robe held Jori's hand as he led her down a corridor in the belly of Morhelgol. Not a soul was around except for the occasional rodent that scurried past their feet. Jori's eyes continually scanned her environment. Her knuckles turned white as she held to the man's hand. The hallway was rather dismal, just more of the same black stone that comprised the rest of the fortress. The flickering torchlight occasionally revealed a painting here or there. Most Jori did not get the chance to look at, but those she did see all seemed to display a running theme of warfare, more precisely a single warrior triumphing.

"Where are we going, Brome?" Jori asked the old man.

"A very special place for only the most special people, my dear. It is down here where I find refuge from the darkness. I have been a servant here for longer than I can remember, and anytime I needed to be alone this, was the place."

"It's so dark down here, and cold. I don't like it." Jori clung closer to the man.

A smile stretched across the old man's lips, though in the darkness, Jori couldn't see it. "Not all darkness is bad, Jori. In fact, it is the light that should fear dark. For dark is inescapable."

"I don't understand. My daddy always said that light drives out the darkness."

"Sometimes, but sometimes the dark gives power to the light, such as when I healed you. I used a magic some would call dark, maybe even bad, but I helped you right?"

"Yes …" Jori said.

"Or how about the times I came to see you when you were crying for your mother? Or when I commanded the osodar to leave the room that one time? Ever since you have known me, have I done anything other than *love* you? I promised you that I would be your friend in this dark place, and I am, but it is by the power of darkness that I am also able to help you through this place."

"So darkness is good? I don't get what you mean."

"Light and dark means more than whether there is light or not, Jori. The day and night difference you experience all the time reflects a deeper truth."

"And nighttime gives you magic?" Jori asked, furrowing her brow slightly.

"In a way. Someday you will understand," the old man said, his smile growing wider.

At the end of the very long hallway, they at last came to a green carpet that lay along the interior of a circular room. As soon as they entered the room, a sudden burst of yellow-white light flashed like lightning then coalesced into a cylindrical green geyser in the center. Jori stopped, staring at the epicenter of the phenomenon she had just witnessed. The green light energy that sprayed from the middle of the room shimmered as Brome walked closer. "Come closer, Jori. Do not be afraid." He motioned, but the little girl simply stood there, slowly shaking her head.

"We should leave. This place is bad," Jori stated, backing up slowly.

"Then just watch." The old man threw back his robe. His skin and eyes blackened as he stuck his hand into the geyser. Beams of radiant green energy engulfed the man, the blackness deepened, his skin cracked, and his hair fell out. After fifteen minutes, the man withdrew his hand from the wellspring of energy. All light disappeared from the room. Then a torch flashed to life, and then another, and another after that until six lights illuminated the chamber once again. Before Jori stood a man she had met before. "Mr. Epsor?" She gasped. "What is going on?" Tears began to flow down her cheeks. "Where is Brome? Where is my friend?"

"That's what I have wanted to tell you, Jori." Epsor smiled. "I am the one you call Brome, I am Epsor, and I am Zontose."

Jori shrieked and turned, running off down the corridor. "Jori, wait!" Zontose screamed. "If I wanted to harm you, you wouldn't be here. You have nothing to fear from me. I have protected you, haven't I?"

"From your own goons!" Jori cried out.

"What people say about me isn't true, my dear. You must believe me."

63

"You murdered my mother and father! I hate you!"

"I didn't kill your parents, Jori. The osodars did."

"But they work for you. Quit lying to me." Jori sobbed.

"Those who were responsible for the terrible deeds that occurred in your village have been punished. I give you my word. The actions of the thworfs and osodars are evil, but they are a means to an end. I want peace. I want this war to end. I have lost people dear to me, too."

"Liar!" Jori screamed and was about to run away, but she was struck with a green blast and collapsed to the ground.

Standing before the girl, Zontose took on the visage of Brome once again and touched Jori on the forehead. "She isn't ready yet," he whispered to himself.

"Where am I?" Jori said slowly. "Brome? Where are we?"

"You must have wandered off, my dear. I was so worried about you. I looked all over the castle for you. It's a good thing I came looking for you; it looks like you hit your head. Here, let me heal it," Brome said, running his hands along her forehead. "Better?"

Jori nodded, and the man helped her up. "Good, now you should go back to your room. You need to take care of yourself."

As Jori lay on her back staring at the ceiling, her breathing was steady and her eyes glistened in the light of a new dawn; a single rivulet from each eye dribbled down her cheeks. "Why haven't You saved me yet?" the girl cried. "Why am I here? Why did You take my mommy and daddy from me? They said You can do anything. They said that You would help me whenever I needed You, but I have asked every day since I got here, and I'm still here. I wanna go home, Lord Voshnore. Brome said that You don't care, that You never help anyone. I said he was a liar, but I don't know now. You are so silent. Please help me; please tell me why I am here." She continued to lie there, staring off, thinking of what her friend said, her parents, the war, and how nothing made sense. As the time passed, Jori felt her mind slipping away to a realm of colors colliding like a pinwheel blowing in the wind. All around, bright hues swirled until they eventually united into a bright landscape. Jori saw herself standing on a shoreline, warm water licking her bare feet as she walked. The sun appeared brighter and larger in the sky, giving her a warm bath in its radiant light. Off to her right lay grasslands that gently blew in the breeze, and beyond that a forest grew. Its bright, spring green reflected so much light Jori found it painful to look upon it.

As Jori walked, her heart beat faster. The smell of life and the warmth made her want to dance and sing. She eventually started humming a tune, but then she saw a transparent figure before her. The figure was female with blonde hair that resembled gold more than what most understand to be blonde. A flowing amethyst robe draped over her moderately-tan skin. Jori jumped backwards, nearly landing on her backside. The woman offered a warm smile and giggled a little, and her form became more solid as she reached out her hand to stroke Jori's cheek. As the woman's form solidified, her skin looked glass-like and flawless. Deep, penetrating, green eyes glinted with both wisdom and love as she smiled.

"Do not be afraid, Jori. You are safe." The woman beamed.

"Where am I? Who are you?"

"I am Vessa, sala warrior of Voshnore. You are on the edge of another realm. By now, I'm sure, you know you are very special because you can see things most others cannot."

"Yes …" Jori said, looking away. "Is that why you are here?"

The sala's brow furrowed. "My precious child, you must be warned. There are dark forces working in the world, and you are in the very center."

"I know, the war," Jori began.

"No, an ancient evil from when the world was younger is coming back and wants you for its own purposes. You must be careful, Jori. You must be careful of Brome," said Vessa.

"Why? He is my only friend."

"He isn't who you think he is," said Vessa. "You cannot trust him."

"What about you? I don't even know you. I prayed to Voshnore every day, and He never answered. Brome came and healed me. He protects me. He is the only one left in the whole wide world who loves me!"

Vessa's brows dropped. Her eyes softened as she met Jori's longing gaze. "Jori, Voshnore has heard every one of your prayers. He has chosen to do something very special for you, but you have to wait. I was sent here to warn you and to give you hope. Voshnore loves you very much. He will save you, but you have been given a choice."

"What choice? Why do you talk like that? I don't know what I'm supposed to do. I don't know if I can trust you or anyone."

"It is for you to find out what the choice is and for you to decide what you feel is right. Remember, Jori, there are consequences for every action, for good or for ill. You were given a marvelous gift, but in order to use it, you must obtain wisdom."

"But I'm just a kid."

Vessa smiled once again. "There is no such thing."

Then Jori's eyes snapped open. The bright, late-morning sunlight shone brightly through the window in her room. Her breathing was labored, and her heart raced. Her eyes wildly darted back and forth. At last, she took a deep breath. "It was only a dream. It was only a dream," she said over and over, but it didn't feel like an ordinary dream to her. Everything was so *real*; there was no sense of relief, only confusion.

# Chapter 6

A city lay sprawled before Aron, stretching farther than he could see. Despite the diminutive size of the ferrorians, the underground city was far larger than any he had seen before. Buildings were constructed out of a green mineral that radiated with an iridescent light. As the knight's eyes beheld the jewel before him, he saw that green, while the dominate color, was not the only one; a few small buildings, which Aron surmised to be houses, shimmered red, orange, yellow, and blue. Everything was smooth. No structure had a right angle or jagged edge. Most buildings were primarily cone or cylindrical in shape, reaching upward to pin-like spires. The ferrorian metropolis looked as if it had been crafted from the most precious of jewels that radiated light of their own. However, that was not the most precarious part of the city. A singular waterfall marked the center of the cityscape. The water, in spite of the green hue of its surroundings, was rust red. Small trees, maybe three- to five-feet tall, with vibrant violet leaves inundated the spaces that were not occupied by the crystalline buildings.

As the two men and the group of ferrorians came closer to the city, sounds of life filled the knight's ears. The wonders of this ferrorian dwelling did not end, for a small creature, maybe six inches long, zipped past his face, and then several more followed. The creatures were tiny golden dragons in pursuit of one another, breathing snippets of fire and rolling around in the air, as if dancing. Aron's eyes followed the golden reptiles with great intensity, observing their whirling loops, undulating spirals, and swiping each other while never harming one another. An utter sense of serenity washed over Aron. The warm light of the minerals, the sound of the rushing water, the bustling of city folk, and the exotic landscape gave no indication of the war ripping apart the surface of Goandria.

The ferrorians led Mathil and Aron to a large gathering placed just outside the city. Tents woven out of some silken material neither man had seen before blanketed the moss-like grasses on the ground. Scattered amongst the tents were ferrorians and humans alike, laughing and talking. Some of the ferrorians even indulged the children by playing games with them.

"I recognize a couple faces." Mathil gasped. "Are these all refugees of Grivear City?"

"Most. Some found their way here from Hallow Forest, but most are survivors like you."

Suddenly, a taller ferrorian draped in a green robe stood up from amongst the crowd and hurried to the newcomers. As the ferrorian came closer, two sky-blue wings tipped with turquoise feathers protruding from his back could also be seen. His wings were folded behind his back, but their size could not be hidden behind his frame.

"Welcome to Untervel, friends! Never before have we sheltered so many humans at once. You are free to stay here as long as you like." The winged ferrorian extended a hand to each of the men.

"Thank you," Aron said, shaking the ferrorian's hand. "My name is Aron, this is Mathil, and we are humbled by your hospitality."

"I am Jennendelf, elder and counselor of the ferrorian peoples," he said, leading the others into a golden tent in the center of the camp.

"This is quite the operation you have here, Jennendelf," Aron commented as they entered the tent. Furniture lined the rim of the tent, which was surprisingly human-sized except for a single armchair in the center. Jennendelf motioned for Aron and Mathil to take a seat. The knight moved over to a sofa and noticed engravings all along its wooden surface. Aron stretched out his fingers over the oak leaf carvings in the arm of a couch. The leafy engraving twisted over the armrest, onto the back, and morphed into a depiction of ferrorians and their dealings with much larger folk. As Aron's eyes continued to examine the design, it further depicted the ferrorian people bowing before the larger peoples then abruptly fleeing and finding a new home beneath the surface.

"This is magnificent artwork," Aron said.

"Yes; it is the story of our people. We engrave it on all our furniture so that we may never forget the sacrifices of our ancestors."

"I didn't imagine your kind making such big chairs and such. I mean ..."

"That's enough, Mathil," Aron spoke up hastily, cutting off the other.

"Oh, it's quite all right." Jennendelf chuckled. "Now, I like to meet with all our guests before they stay. You are welcome to stay as long as you like, but as humans I recommend you don't stay here too long."

Mathil and Aron exchanged glances. "What do you mean?" asked the younger one.

"You have only just arrived, but did you happen to notice anything peculiar about the other ferrorians?"

The two men just shrugged.

"Perhaps, maybe, you have noticed that I am different; that I'm much larger than my kin and have wings?" Jennendelf asked.

"Yes ... What does this have to do with anything? We may stay a few nights, and that's about it; we are merely passing through."

"Wait, *we*? What do you mean *we*? I don't have to go anywhere with you," Mathil protested.

"Fine, stay." Aron shrugged. "My mission was to find survivors of Grivear City and report the damage that was done, and that mission is complete."

"So you aren't refugees, then?" Jennendelf questioned.

"I'm not, but he is," Aron said. "We were fleeing from thworfs when we accidentally came across your city."

Jennendelf nervously scratched the back of his neck. "Well, I suppose I should tell you either way. When we discovered this area, we were much larger than we are now, but as generations passed, those of us who lived into adulthood noticed something. The minerals that give us heat, warmth, light, food, and life have been causing our race to get smaller and less intelligent. We are being poisoned by our life source, and it affects humans much more adversely."

"But there are so many other humans here," Mathil said.

"Yes, and they are aware of the risks, but they prefer that to the war above. Also, I give you this advice so that you may understand my people and have patience with them while you stay."

"Of course, counselor." Aron smiled. "As I said, I don't plan on staying long. Now, if you don't mind, I would like to get some sleep."

"Oh! I'm sorry, I didn't mean to keep you. Come this way." Jennendelf stood up, leading the men outside to an adjacent tent.

"I hope this suffices. It isn't much," the ferrorian said.

"This works for me." Aron shrugged.

"Sure, but it's kinda small," Mathil mumbled under his breath. Aron shot the young man a glare, but Jennendelf didn't seem to notice and quickly took his leave.

Aron wasted no time stretching out on the bed, not even bothering to undress or remove his weapons.

"So what exactly did you do before the war? Um, Aron?" Mathil said, turning to see the knight already asleep. "So much for conversation."

After a long, dreamless sleep, Aron began to stir. He rolled slowly to his left side, and his eyes opened. The knight let loose a great yawn, rubbed his eyes, and then sat up. He found himself alone in the tent. Mathil's bed was tidy as if unused, which Aron found odd but quickly shrugged off. Walking through the tent opening, Aron scanned the immense cavern, slowly looking around, bathing in the new sights before him. He eventually strolled along the outer rim of the city. The closer he came to the rock interior, the more intense the minerals became, not only in light but heat as well. Aron shielded his eyes with his left hand as his gaze traveled upward; he hadn't noticed before, but on the western and eastern sides of the cave, the minerals were unobstructed by other rocks. He chose to travel west, eventually finding a smoothed-out path along the way. Upon closer inspection, he noticed the cavern was comprised of the same jagged rock that lined the tunnels below Grivear City. However, the ferrorians managed to tame the unruly rock, smoothing it out to the appearance of glass. Aron stepped out onto it warily, expecting the surface to be like glass, but he was surprised to find that the tread on his boots gripped firmly.

After walking for some time, Aron hastily sat down and inspected his feet. They had managed to scab over, but some areas had come open again. He grimaced while attempting to stand up again. Pain shot into his calves as he tried to walk for a second time. He wondered why his feet hurt so miserably when just minutes before they were fine enough. Sitting back down, he let loose a sigh and chucked a nearby rock that clanked off a jutting stalagmite. A couple minutes passed. Aron clenched his fists and wobbled to his feet. He managed to take a few steps before falling and slamming his head into a nearby boulder.

When Aron had come to, the first thing he saw were large flaps of canvas draping over the area in which he lay. For a brief moment, he wondered if he had just experienced a vivid dream, but his searing headache reminded him of the reality of the situation. He attempted to turn his head straighter but cried out as white hot pain coursed through his skull, blinding his vision.

"Lay straight. Yes, yes, you must to lay straight!" reprimanded a high-pitched voice from the adjacent section of the tent.

"He messed his leg up good! Yes, he did indeed!" another voice chimed in.

"The caves are very dangerous. You were lucky to be found," yet another ferrorian said.

"What was he doing?" the first one asked.

"Probably looking for a way out."

One of the other ferrorians giggled. "Why do you think that? He came here for sanctuary, yes, yes!"

The knight groaned. Placing his hands on either side of the bed, he shakily raised himself to a sitting position. As soon as he was upright, Aron held his left hand to his temple, massaging it tenderly. Once the throbbing subsided a bit, Aron's vision cleared. A handful of ferrorians hastily hurried to and fro. "What's going on?" Aron asked drearily. Just as the words left his lips, memories of the road inundated his mind: the searing pain in his feet, the inability to walk, and then darkness. Remembering his feet, he quickly looked down to inspect them. Each foot was bound in canvas-like bandages with a green ointment oozing out of the seams. Aron no longer felt pain in his feet. In fact, when he wiggled his toes, he couldn't feel anything. Numbness made its way up to his knees. He tried to move his toes and then his foot, but he could feel nothing. "What's going on? Where am I?"

"Be still! Be still!" a ferrorian responded.

"Your feet! You did not take care in the tunnels, no, no! They have become infected. But do not fret. They

74

will be healed by the end of the day. You are lucky we found you," another one said.

"Here, drink this! You will feel better in a hurry. It will help you sleep, and when you wake, you will be all better!" The first ferrorian shoved a vial of bluish-green liquid in Aron's face. Within a few minutes, deep, dreamless sleep overcame him. When he woke once more, his head no longer throbbed, and the numbness was completely gone. However, as he gazed around, his mind felt foggy, like he had either slept for only a few minutes or way too long. Rubbing his eyes then blinking a few times, he saw another lying in an adjacent bed, maybe five to six feet away, who began to stir as well. "Mathil?" Aron asked slowly.

"Uh …" he groaned, "Ar … on? Where are we?"

"Well, apparently my feet became infected from the minerals in the tunnels, and I'm assuming yours did too. Where were you? Last I saw, you were in our tent, and then you just disappeared."

"Oh, ah, sorry. I went to talk to the other refugees, and I remember my feet started to really hurt, I mean *really* hurt, and after that, I have been in and out of consciousness since, not fully coming to until now. But what I do know is that those ferrorians sure talk a lot! I would catch pieces of their chatter, and my mind would incorporate it into my dreams. I tell you, that was not always very pleasant!"

Aron let out a deep chuckle. "I see you still have a way with words. So are you thinking about staying?"

"I'm not sure." Mathil shrugged. "I don't know, probably not." The youth's eyes angled downward at the floor as he continued. "I'm really sorry about the hard time I gave you. I know you were just trying to do what was best for us, and it all worked out in the end."

Aron's face cracked with a thin smile, and it slowly grew to a full grin. "I appreciate that, Mathil."

Mathil's face contorted a bit. "What?"

"Ah, it's nothing."

"What?" Mathil asked again. "What's so funny?"

"I just had a thought." Aron shrugged. "Was that difficult for you to say?"

"Ah, seriously?" Mathil sighed as he turned away, his face flushed.

"Apologies do not seem to be something you do often, that's all. I don't mean anything by it."

"So what are your plans once you are better?" Mathil asked.

"Oh, well, I still need to give my report to the Republics. The king is probably wondering what is taking me so long. I will eventually return to aiding the warfront." As Aron spoke, his jaw tightened and his eyes burned with a passion.

"You've lost a lot, haven't you?"

A brief silence followed. The knight's eyes did not meet Mathil's as he sat. His breathing was becoming more labored, and his right hand clenched into a tight fist. "Zontose has stolen much from me," Aron said slowly. "I want to see him fall from his throne. I want him to topple from his place of might so that no other may endure what I have, and the longer that takes, the more lives he destroys."

"Then let us do it together. Once we are fully healed, I will go with you and make war upon Zontose."

"It isn't that simple." Aron smiled wearily. "The truth is, neither one of us will ever deliver the final blow to that monster. There are thousands of stories similar to mine and yours. Mathil, you must also understand it is easy to say you will fight, but war is unlike anything you have experienced. Ask yourself if you can truly take a life, if you can hold it together when your comrades are dying all around you. Are you ready to die for what you believe in?"

Mathil's eyes shifted downward, and his lips pursed together. "I guess we are going to find out, but I would like you to teach me how to fight."

"My job was to search for survivors, not train soldiers," Aron stated matter-of-factly.

"You cannot be serious."

"Oh, indeed I am. I am an archris knight, and I have spent years training for war. I do not have the time, nor the responsibility, to train you."

"I have just as much right to fight as you do, Aron. You said it yourself, there are others like us whose lives have been turned upside down from this war. Look at the ferrorians here. They are living in a place that is slowly poisoning them because the surface is torn apart by this war. Goandria is sick, and the best cure is if all who have suffered rise up against Zontose. I will not take no for an answer. I wish to fight and to be taught how to avenge my family."

A slight smile formed across Aron's face. "Then so be it."

The red sands of Dalarashess swirled as hundreds of thousands of thworfs, katzians, and dragons fell into formation. From the summit of Morhelgol, it looked as if countless ants stood awaiting the arrival of their queen. Katzians screamed orders as their leather whips tore into thworf hides. The hordes murmured amongst themselves, some shaking their heads, some grimacing, but then an abrupt silence fell upon the army as horns bellowed. Just beyond the northwestern horizon, a mass of large men mounted upon white warhorses rode forth. Steely brown and blue eyes stared through iron helms which bore an hourglass shape, symbolizing the region they hailed from. Each member was clad in dark green, black, and brown, and strapped to their backs were longbows and broadswords. At the head of each regiment were two katzians, whose armor bore the same insignia. Into the bleak region of Dalarashess they marched, never even glancing at the opposite army. Their chests remained outward and their chins upright.

Zontose emerged from the tower, making haste toward the oncoming army. The leader of the thworfs greeted him with a low bow then proceeded to walk beside Zontose. "Your majesty, are these the reinforcements you promised?" the thworf general asked.

"They are, General Cshar," said Zontose.

"Barbarians from the north?"

"These men are so much more than that, and they have served me well."

The katzian at the front of the new army met Zontose. "Greetings, men of Dalarashess!"

"Hail Zontose!" the army cried out as one.

Zontose raised his hands to the sky, and his body levitated. "I, your master, have summoned you to not only bring war to the oppressive lands to the south, but also to bring a new order and a new way of life. The thworfs, like you, were shunned by the Republics, and now I implore you to be not only brothers in arms but in purpose. That purpose is to wake Goandria from its ignorance, intolerance, and arrogance."

Not all thworfs cheered in response to Zontose's speech. Many murmured amongst themselves as Zontose spoke. Suddenly the dark one fell silent. "Is there someone who would like to speak his mind?" None spoke. Many backed away as Zontose hovered over them. "If there are doubts, please speak up! We do not keep secrets from our new friends."

After several minutes, a large thworf inched toward the newcomers. Smelling the air, he puffed out his chest and tapped one of the soldiers on the head with his sword. "These are our new allies?" the thworf chuckled in a gurgling fashion. "They look even weaker than the dainty soldiers of the Republics!" Other thworfs began to giggle, and then the larger thworf poked at a soldier again. "See fellas …" a flash of steel abruptly whirled through the air, taking the thworf's head off, then stopped as the soldier resheathed his broadsword. A look of horror fell upon the faces of the surrounding thworfs, and they quickly fell back into formation.

Zontose touched down before General Cshar. "I want you to see to it personally that our new guests receive the best arrangements."

"As you wish my lord." The thworf bowed.

"Also, summon the osodars to meet me within the hour. They will know where." The thworf bowed once again as his master turned and made haste for the tower.

Zontose's feet heavily clomped against the stone floor as he marched back into the lowest level of Morhelgol, his servants hastily moving out of his way and bowing as their lord passed. At last he entered the room to which he had brought Jori just a few days prior. The mystical green geyser erupted to life when he set foot in the chamber. This time, however, it gradually expanded, splattering the entire room. Moving to the north end of the chamber, Zontose's hands repositioned his hood. He inclined his chin slightly, raising his hands upward. Along the outer wall of the chamber, seventeen yellow-orange-and-black vortices appeared, manifesting into ghastly figures resembling reanimated, transparent skeletons. Each of them was shrouded in a yellow-orange hue that radiated from their being. Their piercing blue eyes snapped to life as they materialized, then gray robes and black cloaks appeared on each. All osodars faced the central geyser of energy, placing their right arms across their chests and chanting, "Lord of darkness, master of all, guide us and empower us." Then each bowed a knee.

Zontose stood perfectly still for several minutes. Eventually, his head lifted slightly as he lowered his hands, placing his palms upward before him. His blackened lips curled inward, and his crackling voice silently formed the words he desired, "Lahsa ertro pauerrala." He repeated the words of the ancient language, and with each recurrence, his voice grew louder. Green orbs of fire formed within his grasp. After ten times of reciting the incantation, the osodars joined in, each one rising to his feet. A soft thud stomped in the background, sending slight reverberations through the fortress' foundation. The thudding grew in volume, becoming rhythmic in nature and giving the impression of drums beating in the distance. As the tempo increased, lightning crackled from the central column of energy. The green energy contracted, and the lightning blasts became more intense until at last the geyser was no more. Instead, a spherical ball levitated, rising slowly. The chanting continued for several more moments, but suddenly the green sphere exploded into red energy bolts that struck all within the room. As the red lightning coursed through Zontose and his servants, they rose three feet above the stone floor.

Stretching out his arms, Zontose cried out in modern Goandrian, "Return! Arise, mistress of darkness; let us make this world ours!" A terrible scream emanated from the red sphere. Then the ball of energy shook with so much force it seemed that an explosion was imminent. The sphere continued to vibrate until another scream sounded. A black shade emerged from the sphere, raced madly into each wall of the chamber, then collided with the ceiling and floor. The ghastly figure which was birthed from the spherical orb of energy was vaguely human in shape, but tendrils trailed behind in place of legs.

Zontose's eyes followed the entity as it thrashed about. The sphere of energy dissipated, and the unlit torches in the chamber ignited when at last the spirit calmed and hovered motionless where the geyser once flowed. The fire of the torches, fed by dark magic, arced toward the shade, only to be continually absorbed into utter blackness. The entity let loose another scream before it turned to Zontose. Its silvery skull and needle-like teeth were visible for a slight moment in the light from which it fed. "Who … dares?" a deep, scratchy voice asked.

"My mistress, it is I," Zontose replied.

The shade said nothing, moving closer to Zontose and growing in size before it diminished once again, collapsing into a pile of black mist that hovered at his feet.

"Do you not remember me? I showed you the path to ultimate power."

"You … it … cannot … be …" the entity whispered, struggling to regain form, but as more light was syphoned, the mist lifted itself up. The vague outline of a humanoid figure returned.

"How I have waited for this moment. I never forgot you."

"The … *master*?"

"Yes, my queen. I have grown stronger, stronger than ever before. My time has come to at last claim Goandria. There are some who suspect me, but you, you are now lost to history. You shall help me claim this world."

# Chapter 7

Two combatants whirled around one another. In the light of the glowing crystals, sweat glistened on their foreheads as each waited for the other to attack. A few ferrorians perched themselves on nearby rocks to watch. *Tink, clank, clank,* two weapons clashed together. "Move your feet," Aron said as he whirled his sword around.

"Easy for you to say! All I have is this dagger," Mathil breathed. The young man lunched forward with his blade, but the wide attack was easily parried, resulting in Aron's sword tip at his throat.

"You cannot just flail your weapon, hoping that luck will guide it to its target. And your dagger is more than adequate. It nearly qualifies as a short sword."

"Even so, with your weapon being twice the size of mine, it is a little intimidating."

"Do you want to learn or not?" asked Aron as his sword moved in to strike Mathil. The boy quickly parried but was knocked back. "Good! Now again!" Aron smiled as he unleashed a furry of attacks that knocked Mathil off his feet again.

"I think you need to take into consideration I have never done this before …"

"And you need to consider, Mathil, that your enemies will not care. Whether you are a novice or a veteran will not matter in the end. What will matter is who has the advantage."

"But we have been at this for over an hour! When are we going to leave this place?"

"In the morning," said Aron as he levied his blade against Mathil's once more. "For someone who has never had any training, you are doing surprisingly well."

"Well, what do you know, Aron does offer compliments." Mathil smirked.

"I wasn't finished yet. You may have a good start, but you have no technique, your attacks are too wide, and you fight with too much emotion instead of being aware of your bearings." Aron attacked again, hitting Mathil's dagger out of his hand. "And you wonder why I am being so hard on you. If you want to survive, if you want to learn, this is what needs to be done. I asked you if you were ready. I asked you if you really wanted to fight."

Mathil scowled. "You cannot expect me to know everything right away! Yes, I want to learn, but I want my teacher to have patience."

"I already told you …"

"And I told you that I am going to fight against Zontose. No matter what that looks like, I want to be a thorn in his side. I told you that I have just as much right to fight as you do."

Aron's eyes narrowed. He was about to respond, but his ear caught another voice quietly saying, "The humans fight so much. Yes, yes, fighting and bickering and arguing so much." It was a ferrorian's voice speaking to another of its kind. Their wide eyes took in the whole scene before them. For a second, the knight glared at the small creature, who quickly looked away and then got up to leave. The knight simply watched him, his mouth open slightly as he saw the ferrorian walk away. Aron knew what he was doing. His heart thudded a little harder, realizing what was going on.

"You are right, we are done for the day. Make sure you are ready to leave in the morning," Aron said before silently walking back to their tent. His mind went to his own training, how every day had seemed like a brutal punishment. The bruises had covered his arms, legs, and chest, and he had constantly felt inadequate until one day everything clicked and he was finally able to best his instructor. *That is what I was hoping Mathil could feel someday. I want him to know what it is like to overcome such a difficult task, to succeed and become confident in his abilities*, he thought. Then his mind went to Jori. Teaching her how to walk and talk were struggles he helped teach Jori to overcome. He smiled grimly. His daughter had struggled with language for the longest time. He loved seeing her finally get it. He loved to see how she became more confident. "And I'm trying to be a father to Mathil," he said out loud, placing his hands over his face.

Large, bright, yellow-orange eyes peeked from behind a twisted tree trunk. Dozens of her kin huddled inside a pillared, rectangular structure comprised of silver and granite. The roof of the building was golden with silver outlining a massive female warrior. Just outside the entrance, a twelve-foot idol of the same woman stood. The painstakingly-carved stone depicted the woman standing strong. Her bulging muscles flexed as she grasped her spear, and despite the stone, her eyes held a fire within them. Two bells located in a central tower on the roof of the building rang twelve consecutive times with no rhythm or musical beat. Then they abruptly ceased. The observer waited until the temple doors thudded closed before she sighed deeply and darted off further into the woodland. As she ran, the gold and violet leaves on the ground became entangled in her bushy tail and the low branches continually assaulted her from all directions.

At last she came to a very small clearing in the forest. From amongst the woodland on the opposite side of the clearing, another like her emerged. The other was slender and of average height, around five and a half feet tall, with the same dazzling, yellow-orange eye. A coat of yellow, white, and red fur covered her body, and foxlike ears poked out from under locks of blonde hair. "Raskka! You're safe! Did anyone see you?"

"No, Camalyn. They still think I'm ill, but I managed to sneak out after Mother left."

"Are you sure you want to do this? You will be playing a very dangerous game."

"It's a dangerous world. If it isn't those purist radicals, it is Zontose. How long will it be before he notices us and desires to use us, too?"

"Zontose isn't our concern, Raskka." Camalyn lowered her voice to a whisper. "We must sustain our people and our way of life. The humans, thworfs, and even the englifs are our prey. They will fund our fight for freedom to worship the goddess as she decreed to our prophetess."

"I pray that Qunzarrah gives us all strength," said Raskka.

"Come, daughter of the goddess. I want you to meet the others if this is that path you have chosen." A dozen others emerged from the cover of the forest, each bearing two short swords held at the ready. "We will take you to the prophetess herself." Camalyn smiled, placing her right hand on Raskka's back.

The morning sun glistened through the heart of the gold and violet forest canopy, giving the atmosphere a reddish hue. The fourteen companions slinked through the woods, their padded feet enabling them to move swiftly and quietly as they hastened onward. As they made their way into the center of the forest, the overhead canopy allowed for less and less of the sun's rays to reach the ground. *This is finally it!* Raskka thought excitedly. *I am finally going to become one of them and join the true followers of the goddess.*

As they went further into the woodland, a blanket of fog began to appear around their feet, and the sounds of wildlife quickly diminished until all anyone heard was the rustling of the wind. In what Raskka perceived to be the far off distance, branches snapped every so often, and the sound of crushing leaves echoed throughout the woody area. She became acutely aware of her surroundings. The leather she wore squealed annoyingly while she attempted to listen closer. Raskka's heart pounded harder and harder and harder, until she felt as if it was beating within her throat. Wisps of vague shapes and figures periodically zipped by. She could barely see them out of the corner of her eye.

"Are you all right?" Camalyn's voice suddenly cut the silence.

"Huh?" Raskka jumped. "Oh, I uh, I just rarely come this way. I generally stay near the forest edge. I think my imagination is getting the best of me."

"Imagination?" Camalyn's head cocked and one eyebrow went up.

Raskka hastily waved the air. "It's nothing, I'm sure. There is just a strange air here, like there is someone or maybe several people watching us."

"What I meant was, are you sure it *is* your imagination? Have your adventures into the outside world corrupted you so? Have you forgotten the teachings of our ancestors?" Camalyn said, a slight smile forming across her lips.

"What is that supposed to mean, Camalyn? I have forgotten nothing," Raskka protested.

"Are you sure? There are many who would deny the true nature of the goddess, even within our own kin. Beyond our sacred forest, skepticism, false worship, and evil are everywhere. They go so far as to even deny what is so plain before them. Take great care not to stumble into the outside ways. The goddess has no patience or love for the adherents of blasphemy. The people of Goandria have forgotten that another reality exists beyond that which we can see. Have you, in your youth, already succumbed to the foolishness that lies beyond our doorstep?" She received no response.

Raskka could feel her cheeks growing hot and subconsciously bowed her head. *What a start to a new journey,* Raskka thought solemnly. Some of the others noticed Raskka's shame and chuckled a bit to themselves, shaking their heads.

The group reached the very heart of the forest just past sundown, and Raskka soon forgot about the embarrassing reprimand from her friend. Her mind whirled with excitement, contemplating her new spiritual commitment. *Finally, freedom, freedom to embrace the goddess as she designed! I wish my mother would see that the way she follows is*

*not the path of truth. I wish I could convince all of the Qunzarria*
...

Above, bits of evening light streamed through the leafy canopy. The fog was no longer merely knee-deep, but it had slowly encroached upon the entire forest, devouring everything in its wake. Raskka was surprised she hadn't noticed sooner how quickly the fog arrived. It was difficult to see more than a couple feet in any direction. The only things that were clearly visible were the massive, gnarled pillars of the forest. Faint whispers echoed in what seemed to be the far distance of Hallow Forest. The deeper Raskka and the others ventured, the more groaning and faint murmuring could be heard. Raskka's hands balled into fists. Continually checking her surroundings, she wondered if what she was hearing were distant travelers, animals, or her imagination. She felt like there was an army of souls surrounding her, close yet far away. Even more distressing, Raskka could not tell if the voices she heard were in pain, malevolent, or benevolent. No one else appeared to be bothered or to take notice that anything was amiss.

The foliage of the forest was now primarily golden. The canopy allowed slightly more sunlight, giving the foggy atmosphere a golden, iridescent hue. Wisps of formless shadows darted just within Raskka's view. Her pulse sped up, and the hair on the back of her neck stood on end, but she was unsure why or perhaps did not want to entertain the idea forming in the back of her mind. Raskka shut her eyes tightly for a few seconds, and when they reopened, she took a deep breath and resolved to focus on her surroundings.

*The goddess' hand creates such beauty. This forest is unlike anywhere in Goandria. It is the pinnacle of her creation.* Raskka marveled. It was in this area that the forest was tallest, but despite their soaring heights, the trunks were only about two feet in diameter. Large, black vines zig-zagged along the ground, enveloping a quarter or so of the trees. Here, Camalyn signaled the group to halt. "We are close now. My fellow sisters, this place Qunzarrah made to be a refuge for us, her chosen ones. This, the golden realm of the Hallow Forest, is where her realm, the realm of the goddess, the god, and the spirits, is most thinly separated from the realm of the physical. We renounce the blasphemies of the Qunzarria, who dogmatically state that the goddess may only be worshipped in their temple. Can a bottle contain the wind? How then should any expect that our beloved mother be contained in a temple? We, the Sul-Qunzarria, will worship her as she intended, free from the confines of a temple, wherever we may choose." For a moment, Camalyn was silent, and great wings of orange fire extended from her shoulderblades. The flames crackled a bit as they devoured the air around them like a campfire, and the more oxygen they absorbed, the redder the fire became. "We have been given the power to take what we will for the glory of the goddess!" Camalyn continued, and her wings flared as her voice grew more intense. "All are our prey, humans and thworfs particularly, but most of all, our own kind who have cruelly tortured and executed those who disagree with them."

A loud cheer erupted from the others. "Let us glorify the goddess and show the people of Goandria that *we* are the chosen ones! We will show the world that we will not succumb to this petty war. The frushian people are strong. We are survivors!"

One of the others stepped forward and interjected, "I saw that a couple of men have wandered into our forest while on our way to our new sister."

Raskka's eyes darted from the one who spoke to Camalyn. Camalyn puffed out her chest, curling her lips. "You all know what we do with intruders." Manifesting wings of their own, each frushian shot skyward in a blazing streak.

"You know, I can't believe I ever entertained the idea of taking up permanent residence in Untervel. The refugees must have nerves of steel to spend all day every day with those blasted ferrorians!" Mathil said, half chuckling to himself.

"Oh, come now. They weren't *that* bad. They did help us, after all. Maybe you should be a little more grateful," Aron countered.

"Jennendelf said this passage would come out at the very edge of Hallow Forest. We have been walking for over an hour."

"Yes, he did. Just be patient," Aron said.

"Does anything make you want to hurry? It would sure be nice to see the outside world again, although Hallow Forest is not exactly high on my priority list."

"I see you are back at it again, Mathil." Aron shook his head.

"What?"

"Complaining about everything."

"I'm not complaining!"

"If you say so." Aron shrugged.

"And I am grateful. For being odd little fellows, the ferrorians sure are good healers. I just don't understand knowingly exposing themselves to poisonous minerals like that."

"Jennendelf already explained that," Aron said.

"He did. He and his people elected to poison themselves instead of taking a stand."

Aron stopped. The knight's dark eyes met the young man's. "As hard as it may be for you to believe, Mathil, you cannot see all ends. The ferrorian people have a right to choose their own fate. What chance would they stand against Zontose's armies? It is not our place to criticize them."

"You're so quick to jump down my throat!" Mathil retorted. "I don't know what the answer is, obviously, but I just can't see the logic in what they are doing. Anyone can see that!"

Aron sighed again. "Yes, it seems strange to someone on the outside, and I'll give you that. The fact remains that they showed us nothing but kindness when we least expected it." Aron turned and continued walking. "They even gave us directions to the surface so we don't have to face those blasted tunnels and their sharp stones."

"No, instead we are traveling in yet another tunnel with stones smoothed out by the little people."

Aron snorted slightly. "I don't even know why I bother." The glittering minerals in the stone brightened as the two of them continued onward. The tinted light revealed Mathil's downward brows, squinted eyes, and pursed lips. Aron nearly laughed at the sight. A half hour passed before the familiar yellow light of the sun gleamed into the cavern.

"You see that too, Aron? Tell me it's real! Oh, beautiful sunlight! It feels like I haven't seen it in months!" Mathil exclaimed, charging full on toward the exit. Bursting out of the small cavern, Mathil stretched his hands upward, giggling madly as he jumped up and down over and over.

When the knight emerged, he quickly shielded his eyes, squinting while they adjusted. He glanced at Mathil for a moment, slightly shaking his head. They were in a rectangular field littered with tall brown and green grasses. Red and orange flowers spotted the ground every so often. Fifty feet in front of the cave's mouth and twenty-three feet behind, massive walls of gnarled trunks rose. High above, the westerly wind tussled the golden and violet foliage. Aron took in a deep breath, and a smile crossed his face as he exhaled. His head turned upwards as his brown eyes scanned the immense forest, resting on the glittering leaves. "Nowhere have I seen such beauty. It is nice to be back," Aron muttered under his breath.

Mathil halted awkwardly, looking over his left shoulder. "Huh? You say something?"

Aron's lips formed a half-smile. "Naw. Wow, you really get over-excited, don't you?"

"Uh, I guess. Not usually, though. Aren't you happy to finally be above ground?

"I am, I am, but I didn't think you wanted to come here."

Mathil's face scrunched up for a second. "What do you mean?"

"Hallow Forest," Aron said, raising his hands with his palms upward.

"Oh, I uh, yeah. Well, let us hope that the stories about this place aren't true."

"What stories?"

"In Grivear City, many of my peers said that this place is haunted and that there is a race of crazy people that steal and murder those who venture too far into the forest," Mathil said.

"Hmm, strange. I've never heard such tales, and I have been here before, long ago when I was studying to become a knight. I did not come across any such things or see any signs of the forest being haunted, but of course we also did not venture very far in. The Hallow Forest can be treacherous even without ghosts; the dense forest makes it easy to get disoriented."

"You know, that isn't any more reassuring, Aron. Do you even know where we are?"

Aron took in a deep breath. His eyes scanned the area one more time before he spoke. "No, I have never heard of a clearing by a cave in the forest before. Of course, like I said, I didn't venture in horribly deep. This time, it looks like we have little choice if we wish to reach Hondor at all."

"Which way do we even go?"

"Hondor is east from Grivear City, so it would be that way," Aron said, pointing behind him and to the right of the cave. "Are you ready for this?"

"Like you said, what real choice do we have? Poisoning ourselves with the blissful little people or a dense and endless wilderness. Hmm, I guess the forest it is!" Mathil said.

The dead leaves on the forest floor crunched beneath the soles of their boots. The fallen leaves were dried, rust-colored, shriveled husks of their former glory, yet there was a small remnant of a speckled sheen locked inside. *It is like the forest's beauty cannot diminish, no matter what happens,* Mathil noted, gazing at his feet. His eyes were cold and narrow, soaking in the wonder of Hallow Forest. *Still, the beauty of this place does not make it any more comfortable to be in,* he mused to himself.

As they moved onward, their breathing became more labored, for the air quickly became denser the deeper they went into the forest. The amount of trees increased in this region, as if the woodland had sought to cover every inch of empty space, and where there were no trees, black vines ensnared the rest of the area. This situation provided very little room for the travelers to continue onward. Determined, Aron pressed forward, unwilling to submit to the harshness of the terrain. He continually looked to the sky, checking the trunks of the trees and the ground as they trekked. Occasionally, the knight would get down on all fours, carefully brushing his fingertips along the ground before silently moving on. Mathil quietly questioned what the other was doing, often sighing during Aron's frequent stops, but he decided to not say anything about it. The young man did not have a clue how to navigate the forest, and he prayed Aron's archris knight training provided that.

It wasn't long before the sun began to set. The evening light failed to pierce the forest canopy, but a dazzling array of colors glinted from above. A billowing white blanket came down from the northern area of the woodland, washing over the entire forest floor. In a matter of moments, the swirling vapor rose, steadily climbing up the tree trunks to their branches until it blanketed the men's vision above them as well.

"Where did all this fog come from so fast?" Mathil said.

"I, I don't know. I have never seen anything like it."

"The sun has set, and now it is incredibly foggy. What do we do now?"

"We make camp here for the night," Aron responded.

"Is it safe? I don't know what it is, but I've got a bad feeling, and it's more than just the stories I have heard."

Aron's eyes squinted. "Me too, but maybe it's just the uncertainty of this place. There are a lot of mysteries here."

Mathil groaned. "I guess we should build a fire then. At least we can be warm if we are stuck."

Aron's hand grabbed Mathil's shoulder. "No. I don't think there are ghosts here, but there may be other dangers. I think it would be unwise to draw any unnecessary attention to ourselves. There may be unknown predators that roam these woods."

Mathil groaned even louder this time. "Of course!" He sprawled out his cloak on the ground and curled up on it. Aron quickly followed suit, closing his eyes. Sleep overcame him in spite of the cold, hard ground. Mathil, however, lay on his back, wide-eyed and clutching his tattered cloak about him. Clatters and groans, shrieks and creaks filled the forestland. After a few minutes, Mathil attempted to lay on his left side, using a nearby tree branch as a pillow. He closed his eyes.

The creaking timber seemed to grow louder. In the distance, a monotonous wail emanated. Mathil took in a few deep breaths, but his heartbeat felt like the whole world could hear it. *I'm just paranoid,* Mathil thought to himself over and over. Eventually weariness overcame anxiety, and he was on the threshold of sleep when a loud shriek, followed by what sounded like a distant dialogue, suddenly echoed again, closer than before. Mathil's eyes snapped open, his hands madly feeling for his dagger. His left hand grasped the cold leather hilt as he drew it close to his breast.

"Aron!" Mathil whispered, "Aron! Aron! Did you hear that? Aron!" The knight did not stir.

Mathil's bulging eyes scanned his surroundings over and over, but he could see and hear nothing. No cricket chirped, no frog croaked. There was absolute silence save for a slight breeze tussling leaves on the highest parts of the trees. *Ugh, I must be losing my mind!* He shook his head as he slumped down against the roots of the tree. Again he inhaled and exhaled slowly, but his pulse refused to quiet. Mathil stared off into the forest. There was nothing but towers of tree trunks as far as the eye could see in the darkness. The young man sighed and closed his eyes, but after a few moments, his ear picked up a faint sound, and then it grew closer and closer. Keeping his eyes shut, Mathil took in several more deep breaths. "I'm only imagining it," he said over and over, but then he faintly heard "*Mathil!*" in his left ear. His whole body spasmed with fright as he jumped to the right. Before him stood a vague figure outlined in a blue radiance. The being had no form that Mathil could accurately compare it to. The youth's throat tightened, and his jaw clenched as he stared at the slender being that remained steady for a moment. Mathil looked closer, tilting his head to the left slightly. The thing before him did not move but simply hovered where it was. *Maybe it's an illusion.* Mathil pondered as he gazed upon it, but then the thing suddenly shifted, and cold rushed down his spine. He wanted to cry out, but his mouth wouldn't open. He dared not swallow, for he feared that the being would somehow hear it. His very blood felt like ice pumping through his veins, and all he could do was collapse onto the ground and cover his eyes with the cloak. *What am I doing? I need to get out of here! But Aron is out cold. I can't survive without him, but we can't stay here either. Oh, Lord Voshnore, help me! Protect me!* He closed his eyes tightly while he continued to pray.

"Mathil? Hey, Mathil! How long are you going to sleep?" Aron's voice broke through. "Come on, get up. It's already late!" He nudged Mathil with his foot.

"Hmm," Mathil groaned, slowly rolling onto his back. His eyelids cracked open a bit and then quickly pressed shut as he rolled back to his side.

"Oh, no you don't!" Aron called out, this time shaking Mathil's torso.

"Agh, come on, I didn't sleep well last night, and it's so bright."

"If you ever want to get out of this forest, we need to get moving, and that means now!"

Mathil's eyes widened, noticing his surroundings. He picked up the dagger he had held all night and slowly replaced it in its scabbard. Once Mathil finished gathering his cloak and his small pack of provisions from the ferrorians, the two men continued onward through the forest. Hours passed, and there appeared to be no break in the trees. Black vines engulfed much of the base of the forest the deeper they traveled, but fortunately so did wild berries during a little over a mile of their journey. The spherical, yellow-orange fruit dangled from knee-high plants between the massive arms of the vines, providing some much needed food.

"Quill berries," Aron said as he picked a handful off a bush. "If only the people of the Republics knew how bountiful they were here, they wouldn't drain so much of their coffers for these things. Look at all of them! I never knew so many grew in one area."

"Yeah ..." Mathil said quietly.

"Wouldn't you like some? You missed breakfast with me, and I haven't seen you eat in ... when was the last time you ate?"

"Sure, I'll take some," Mathil stated simply, grabbing a few from the other's hand.

Little more was said between the two as they walked. Aron's mind reeled as his eyes took in the voluptuous woodlands, but Mathil could not shake the events of the night before. His eyes felt heavy, begging him for the chance to be closed, and his head felt foggy and achy. The ghastly vision replayed in Mathil's mind. His entire body trembled, his heart beat faster, and his fingernails dug into his palms. Then his eye caught something streaking past the small breaks in the tree canopy. Mathil rubbed his eyes. *Ugh, not again,* he thought glumly, but then several more bright red lines followed. Aron didn't seem to notice anything, so Mathil just shrugged it off and kept moving.

Eventually the travelers came upon a narrow pathway that wound through the woodlands. Tall grasses and various weeds poked through the fallen leaves that blanketed the trail. It hardly qualified as a trail, but it was a welcome break in the trees. "We can rest here for now," Aron said, sitting down against a tree. Mathil slowly did the same.

"You okay?" Aron asked after several minutes went by.

"Huh?" The other jumped. "Why do you ask?"

"You usually have much more to say. You said something about not sleeping well last night?"

"I would rather not talk about it," Mathil said sharply, turning around and closing his eyes.

Aron did not press the matter further. He gazed at Mathil, running his left index finger along his mustache, which had grown rather long and unruly. It was the first time he even noticed his facial hair, other than knowing that shaving it was not an option lately. Both hands ran along the four inches of scruff. Occasionally his thumb and forefinger would find a knot or remnant of food that became buried. *Nina would have* … he thought for a moment and then stopped. His brow furrowed, and his gaze deepened. For a brief second, Aron's eyes shifted skyward, then he shook it off and closed his eyes. When they reopened, he turned to talk to Mathil again, but the feel of cold thin steel against his neck stopped him.

"Don't move," said a female voice. Aron slowly turned his head. A person of average height with long, dark-brown hair held the blade to his throat. Her body was covered with a coat of dark yellow and white fur, and two small, canine-like ears protruded from her brown locks. His eyes locked onto the creature before him, attempting to discern what exactly it was. Several others came forth from the woodland behind them with thin, wedge-shaped short swords in each hand. The one with the blade against Aron's throat motioned to them. "Check him," she commanded, and another with more reddish-yellow fur began ruffling through Aron's layers of clothing, painstakingly prodding each nook and cranny. The knight's sword and dagger were the first to be pilfered, along with a few hunting knives and his nearly-empty coin pouch.

"You will find I do not have much of value to you," Aron said, eyeing the women carefully.

Another with long, dazzling blonde hair came over and withdrew Aron's sword from its scabbard. The blonde one ran her fingers along the shiny blade and then suddenly gasped as the weapon fell from her hand. "Camalyn!" she cried out. "He is an archris knight!"

"So? Look at him, Raskka. He is at our mercy, no matter who he is," Camalyn sneered.

"Are you sure?" Aron rammed his elbows into the two that were checking him over, and, like lightning, he proceeded to kick another in the gut, relieving her of her weapons. Two others rushed in, but Aron whirled his daggers around, parrying his opponents before swiftly stabbing one in the chest and another in the neck. Those who were searching Mathil charged at the knight, but instead of grasping their blades, they proceeded to rub their palms hastily, producing bright embers. The red-orange embers burst into a more yellowish flame, and with a shoving motion from the wielders, a blast of fire shot toward Aron's face, barely missing him. Brilliant blasts of fire erupted from the remaining creatures' shoulderblades, coalescing into wings of red-orange. Camalyn's mouth turned upward as she let out a snarl. "You are out of your depth, archris knight. We clearly underestimated you, but the same can be said for us. You and your friend are curious men." She turned to her companions. "Bind them. We will bring them to the prophetess."

Blindfolded and bound tightly with thin rope, Aron and his companion were jerked around like dogs on leashes. Every couple of minutes, sharp tugs on their ropes pulled the men left, right, or forward as a hint to pick up the pace. After a series of jerks, Mathil grunted, resulting in a swift blow to his face. *Seriously? What is their problem? I didn't even say anything*, he thought bitterly. Neither had any idea how long they had been on the march, but what they did know was their feet were killing them. "Can you slow down? Where are you off to in such a hurry?" Mathil protested several times, but every plea for respite or change of pace was met with another hit in the face and their captors pushing them on even faster.

After much time had passed, Mathil's relentless complaints resurfaced again like clockwork. Aron shook his head. "Mathil, maybe you just need to stay silent."

"We don't deserve this! Who do these *things* think they are?" Mathil sneered. His comment was met with the tip of a metal blade poking him between the shoulderblades.

"You should listen to your murderous friend over there," a harsh voice hissed.

"Did you forget who attacked whom? And I wouldn't say we are *friends* exactly, more like …"

"Shut up!" the one behind Mathil snapped, digging her dagger just far enough into his flesh to draw blood.

Suddenly, the company yanked Mathil and Aron to a halt, and their bonds and blindfolds were removed. It was night, but dozens of red, orange, and yellow lights disrupted the blackness. As the two men's eyes adjusted, they saw that the source of the lights were creatures akin to their captors. A few of these beings had fiery wings extending from their shoulders, and others grasped orbs of flame in their palms, ready to hurl them at a moment's notice. The fire light danced against the forest's trunks, and the sparkling foliage glimmered like starlight. All attention was on Camalyn's company as they neared. The strange group of beings gathered between two knolls in the forest. Some stood on planks in the trees, and others were chanting around a statue as their companions approached. Near the center of the valley, between the knolls, stood a taller member of their race. She was draped in a glittering gold and white dress, and a crown of small purple flowers wrapped around her gray head. She approached her kin, looking over the strangers. Turning to Camalyn, she said, "Who are these men you bring to our sacred place? Speak quickly, Camalyn, before the wrath of the goddess comes upon you for your disgrace."

"Prophetess," Camalyn said, bowing low, "one of our sisters spotted these men in our beloved forest. We had …"

"I said be quick about it," the prophetess barked again.

"This one fought back." She shoved Aron forward. "He killed two of our beloved sisters. The law deems …"

"Do not quote the law to me. I wrote it!" snapped the prophetess. Her eyes narrowed as she looked over the two men, then she grabbed Aron's face between her thumb and index finger. "Male filth." She spat at his feet. "You probably do not know what you did in killing our kind. We are the frushians, the chosen people of the illustrious Qunzarrah."

Aron's dark eyes held the woman's, but he did not respond.

"Do you have nothing to say?" she pressed, digging her fingernails into his flesh.

"I do," Mathil called out. "Is what you said supposed to mean something to us? I can't speak for him, but I have never seen your people before, and as for this Qunzarrah, what kind of name is that? And who are you people? You attempt to rob us and then make us out to be the bad guys. What is the deal here?"

The prophetess' eyes narrowed and her head tilted slightly to the right. "How dare you insult the powers that govern the world? Ignorant child, you deserve what's coming to you. Do you know why my sisters brought you and the knight before me?" Her question was met by silence as Mathil's eyes locked onto the ground. "The law of the goddess decrees that any who spill the blood of a frushian must be brought before the priestess to be judged. Qunzarrah commands that fair judgment must be passed, but typically the consequence for such act is death. None of our kind has been murdered in several decades. We take what we need to survive. Few fight back, and even fewer manage to kill any of us. You people are a parasite, taking from the land but never giving back! Your war is tearing Goandria apart. All the while, you justify your actions, saying this war is to eliminate evil. Tell me, what makes you less evil than Zontose? Your vile words and this man's cruel acts tell me you aren't. You say my raiders attacked you first? Maybe that is so, but you are in *our* land, and this forest was given to us by the goddess. You would do well to remember that." After a brief moment of silence, she slapped Mathil. "What does the big-mouthed fool have to say for himself?"

Light-footed Raskka steadily came forward, laying a hand on the prophetess' shoulder, but she was met with slap across her own face as well. Raskka held her reddened cheek. Her eyes widened and her brows narrowed as she stumbled backwards. The prophetess' face twisted and her lips curled, revealing long, pointed teeth. "Raskka! Has their ignorance infected you as well? By what authority do you have the right to interfere with this affair, let alone touch one who is holy?"

"Forgive me, but you need …"

"And now you try to tell me what I need?" The prophetess' eyes widened.

"You cannot tell me this is the will of the goddess, priestess. I joined the Sul-Qunzarria just days ago in hopes to discover the richness of the goddess' beauty. Maybe the Sul are shunned so much because of how radical they are. The goddess can indeed be worshipped anywhere, all is hers. But this, this is a part of the Sul that Camalyn never mentioned. Your temper is like a man's, maybe even worse!"

"Raskka, calm down. You don't know what you are saying. The prophetess commands the will of the goddess. It may be hard to understand, but this is the truth," Camalyn said gently.

"And the priestesses in the temple claim the same thing! Camalyn, you are blinded by this woman! She is no spokeswoman of the goddess! We attacked these men, and the prophetess will not hear them out. What happened to our laws of taking only what we need and not murdering outsiders?" Raskka asked.

"Raskka, we take from the inferior fools who dwell within man's world. We are sacred, and they are not!"

"Quiet, girl!" the prophetess suddenly snapped. "You speak of things beyond your comprehension, Raskka. If you feel so much pity for these killers, maybe you would like to share in their fate?"

"So we are talking about execution? We may be the chosen ones of the goddess, but didn't she create all life? Aren't all living things precious to her? My mother was right. You people are zealots," Raskka snarled.

"Get her out of here before she gets a knife through her heart!" the prophetess commanded.

"Come on, Raskka. I think you have said enough," Camalyn said, laying a hand on the other's shoulder. "I'll take you to my tent and give you time to calm yourself so you can think more clearly."

Raskka looked back over her shoulder at the two men, then furrowed her brow and bowed her head as she was led away.

The prophetess turned her attention back to the men. "Lock them away. They will meet their fate tomorrow."

The men's eyes met for a brief moment, and before they knew it, a sharp blow hit each on the back of the head, rendering them unconscious.

# Chapter 8

The small carriage rocked back and forth as it wound around a maze of corners on the dusty road. The vehicle glittered in the morning sun. As the wheels spun faster around each turn, they sparkled in a yellow-orange blaze. From within the brown, leather-upholstered interior, the sole passenger's rosy, bloated face peeked. "What is taking so long, Hector? We should be there by now. You said one hour, yet the hour has come and gone!"

"Apologies sire," the driver responded, laying a half-dozen more lashes across the four horses' backs.

The woodland along the roadway began to thin quickly, giving way to a sprawling field. Tall, light-brown grasses billowed in the gusts of air the carriage sent as it passed. A herd of spiral-horned buffalo grazing in the grass fields stared hypnotically at the disturbance, then abruptly bounded off westward. The road snaked its way around large hills and wound to the southwest, leading to a wall of stone which reflected the sunlight like a mirror of silver. Within the mirrored walls, white towers rose skyward, built with marbled pillars. The pillars' bronze rooftops tapered to a needle-point and appeared as if they would scratch the puffy, dark gray clouds rolling in from the east. Vague splotches of greens and reds, and perhaps violet but Hector could not be certain, draped down the sides of the pointed towers. As the steeds drew the vehicle nearer, his eyes caught not only the lofty towers, but rocky hill-like formations that periodically rose and fell behind the shimmering walls.

About half a mile before the walls of the city, Hector pulled on the reins, slowing the steeds to a trot. In front of the carriage rose an archway fifty feet across and six feet deep. On either end of the arch stood granite pillars that were roughly seven feet in diameter with simple rope and wood ladders on either side. Curving around the pillars rushed what remained of the river Abahien. Four spearmen guarded the archway on the road, and ten bowmen perched on top. Large steel helms covered the motionless soldiers' faces. The driver inhaled deeply, subconsciously holding his breath as the vehicle passed beneath the crumbling, moss-covered arch. However, his carriage was unhindered by the guardsmen, who abruptly knelt upon seeing the vehicle. Hector sighed, and his tension subsided. Fortune once again smiled upon the driver as the gates to the city opened without him having to stop and introduce his passenger.

Within the walls, a dazzling array of colors greeted the carriage. All shades of greens, reds, oranges, yellows, and violets marked the lush gardens that sprouted atop buildings, on hillsides, at the feet of towers, and on every area that was not consumed with structures. Silver-blue streams of water fell from the tallest buildings into the hands of the shortest, arching until the water emerged through an aqueduct in the walls. The gentle sound of water continually splashing against stone and earth was heard throughout the entire city, and the smell of rain never truly disappeared.

Three squads of soldiers marched in unison, flanking a man and a woman who were adorned with black fur robes. The woman had a slender, amethyst dress, and the man wore a green tunic with gold embroidery in the shape of a magnificent bird with outstretched wings. The man and woman each took to one knee as the carriage rolled to a stop before them. Their ruby-studded, gold crowns dazzled in the late morning light.

Hector hurriedly stepped down, swung the carriage door open, and immediately bowed low. A large mass of human flesh stepped forth from the vehicle. Every ounce of the man jiggled as his stubby legs planted themselves on the ground. He inhaled deeply then released a prolonged exhale. "Perfect, Hector," the man said sarcastically. "It only took forever to get here, and I'm hungry." Hector looked up, his mind sifting through all he desired to say. The man before him hovered like a shadow as his deep green eyes pierced the driver's.

"Sire, I came here as fast as I could," Hector pleaded.

"Oh, I'm sure, but it wasn't fast enough, wonder boy," the other taunted. Everyone within eyesight of the huge man took to one knee, staring at the scene unfolding before them. Once the large man looked at them, the populace immediately diverted their eyes. He grabbed the diamond-and-emerald-studded gold crown from his head, wiped his forearm across his brow, and turned to his hosts.

"Welcome to Belthora, King Ivo." The man and his wife rose to greet the large man.

"Yes, a lovely city you have here, King Locke," Ivo returned the greeting, locking eyes with the other king.

"What brings the High King of the Republics from Hondor in the midst of these dire times?"

"Yes," Ivo said, staring off at the city before him. "I come here personally so you know how important my message is, and I honestly hate being followed by an entourage. I mean, what draws attention more than squads of soldiers following me around?"

*And a gold and silver carriage doesn't?* Locke thought. "What is your message, then?" he asked.

"The world is wearing out. Our wonderful civilization is falling to our enemy fast, and the end of the world as we know it is coming, Locke. We may have been beaten back in the last year, but that devil Zontose wishes to finish us off."

After a short pause, Locke said, "I don't follow your meaning."

"My scouts have reported an army marching to our cities from 33Dalarashess. Battle is upon us, Locke, and we must prepare for one final push before we die."

"An army?" gasped Locke's whiff. "How many are we talking?"

"Somewhere between thirty and forty thousand according to the reports," Ivo said solemnly. He glanced uneasily at the crowd around him. "Is there somewhere else we can talk?"

"Let's go to my palace. You won't have to worry about unfriendly ears there," Locke suggested.

Ivo and Locke strode toward the southern end of the city along a wide roadway that carved right through the heart of the marketplace. Before them stood a dazzling white tower. Its slender, cylindrical formation climaxed to a domed summit, and no seams could be seen in the masonry. It appeared to be formed from a single stone. Flying buttresses emerged from the tower's face, arching to four smaller towers that were each draped with waterfalls. The sun glinted off stained glass windows in the front and sides of the main structure. Human-sized statues lined the walkway to the rounded oak door, each carved in the form of armored men with right hands raised and left hands pointing swords downward.

"Your majesty," Locke said abruptly, "I assure you that you may speak freely here, but if you don't mind, I would rather walk as we converse. It gets stuffy inside." He inhaled deeply, gently closing his eyes. "I find the palace gardens to be soothing, and that is something we all could use in these troubled times."

Ivo's deep brown eyes silently scanned Locke's before he sarcastically said, "Perfect." Ivo rolled his eyes. Ivo's blood felt hot. His heart beat faster, pounding against his ribs. Locke noticed a slight tremble overcome the large man, but he said nothing. They continued to walk along a path in silence, stone soldiers guarding their thoughts and steps. After some time, Ivo's voice sounded. "I have desired nothing more than to protect our people. I ... I ... Uh, met with Zontose to try to negotiate peace."

Locke stopped. His brows narrowed, and his eyes widened as he clasped his left hand on Ivo's shoulder. "You did what? No one has ever been able to talk peace with that man. In the early days of the war, envoys would be sent to find out why he was even warring against us in the first place. They all came back with their heads in a cart. How did you escape?"

"You have to understand, Locke, that this was never my intent. I wanted to protect my girl. I have wanted to keep her in my arms as long as I could ever since the day she was born, but then this war came, and nothing was certain any more. I did something horrible, Locke. I did not escape Zontose. He let me go, and he believes we are allies."

"Ivo, what did you do?"

"About a month ago, I sent word to Dalarashess that I wanted to negotiate with him. I sent a scroll with my servant stating that I understood the Republics had lost. I was willing to do whatever it took to prevent more bloodshed. I was astounded when he consented to meet with me. However, I was not able to travel to Morhelgol right away. After a little over two weeks, my driver discretely escorted me to Zontose's realm. I told my guards that I was coming here and said that having an envoy to protect me wasn't necessary, in spite of their protests.

"When I came to Dalarashess, it was unlike any other place in Goandria. There was red earth as far as I could see and thousands of thworfs. Tall black figures greeted us and demanded to know who I was and what business I had with Zontose. The creatures had large eyes that glowed blue. I felt as if I was standing there naked before them, and my breath was like ice in my lungs even though the heat in that land was utterly unbearable." A small shiver ran through Ivo as he spoke. "I was led by several thworfs and one of those creatures to Zontose's personal chambers. I ... it ... it was so dark in there. The darkness was ubiquitous, despite the torches on the walls. In that instant I wanted to flee, but my legs would not let me. Then I saw him, hooded and armored in black steel. He just stood there watching. I could not see his face, but I felt as if he was smiling, reveling in a moment of victory as his enemy wanted nothing more than to cower from him.

"Zontose bid me welcome and proceeded to ask me what sort of terms I had in mind. I told him I was willing to do whatever it took, as long as my people were safe, even if that meant surrendering our armies to him. He silently watched me, and then a chuckle burst out of him. Zontose asked if I was willing to sacrifice every remaining archris knight to him by allowing his thworfs into Hondor and Belthora to execute each and every knight.

Ivo faced Locke. "I agreed to his terms. As I left, I realized that I had willingly consented to an invasion force to destroy what was left of my beloved Republics. Once we were safely out of Dalarashess, I knew I had done something terrible. Zontose was not going to spare anyone. He was toying with me."

"From what you told me, it doesn't look like you betrayed us. You nearly did, but as you just said, Zontose was toying with you," said Locke.

A large grin unexpectedly formed on Ivo's lips. "How perfect, even you cannot see it!" Then the high king stormed off.

Later that evening, Ivo sat alone in the dining hall. A large piece of cake lay before him with a silver and gold tankard of ale. The table was over twenty feet long and five feet wide, rimmed with chairs all around, but the only people present were two guardsmen in front of the doorway who were still as statues. As he sat there, his left hand stroked the rolls around his massive chin. He spooned a piece of cake into his mouth. Gagging a bit, Ivo used a couple drafts of ale to wash down the cake then followed it with another large spoonful. A few torches illuminated the dining hall, revealing the red and blue tapestries bearing the insignia of Belthora: a silver city radiating from a blue or red background. For a moment, Ivo wondered why Hondor or Grivear City never celebrated their capitals like Verntail. "I suppose it doesn't matter anymore," he said solemnly to himself, letting out a long sigh. *Soon darkness will be upon us, the last stand of the great Republics before they are no more, and it is all my fault. Poor Locke cannot see it, or he chooses not to see it, or maybe he fears that I will charge him with treason if he shows anything but loyalty to me. But treason is what I deserve, for that is what I have committed against the greatest nations that ever were.*

For a moment, his eyes glistened as he stared off into the darkness. *What if this does not have to be so bad? The world is falling apart as it is. The end is coming, and there is nothing anyone can do about it anyway. What if the coming army is not a bad thing? Surely the odds are that we will be crushed, but what if we succeed? It would give us a fighting edge against Zontose. He may even be forced to retreat. Or maybe Zontose will reward me if the Republics do fall. He has no idea that I told Locke of his plans. Then what about Lordrie? I do not know how to keep her safe from this coming battle. I was a fool to think I could trust Zontose. What am I thinking?* Ivo continued in thought, his mind engaging in a tug-of-war.

"Your majesty!" A soldier abruptly burst through the doorway.

"Perfect, a dimwit comes and interrupts my eating!" Ivo barked

"Zontose's army is moving quickly. It is hard to guess how many ... but it seems they will be here within three days, sire. We must prepare the city and send word out for aid."

"Send word? Wonderful! To whom? Do you have any more brilliant suggestions for your king?" Ivo asked slowly. "The wizards, for some reason, will not get involved. Caldaria's englifs cannot reach us in time. Larchrist hasn't lifted a finger to help us. Why should we expect anyone to come? The truth is that the Republics have been on their own since Zontose first assaulted us, and we must fend him off ourselves or be destroyed trying."

A stained-glass window filtered the moonlight into streams of dark red, yellow, and blue, glinting off a man's face as he neared the decoration. The glass outlined the shape of a tall, armored figure, all in black and gray. The figure's helm concealed his face save for a pair of glistening green eyes. A blood red sword dangled from his belt, and the sky around the warrior was amethyst and orange. The dark one's fingers traced the outline of the warrior as a thin smile formed on his lips. The army had marched forth to bring about the final destruction of the Republics hours ago. His spies already reported that Ivo had a change of heart. *No matter. They do not have the strength to repel such an army.*

The room's doors abruptly creaked open, shaking Zontose out of his thoughts. Two thworfs, which stood nearly as tall as the doors themselves, escorted an osodar inside. The creature halted upon seeing Zontose and bowed to the ground immediately. "Daest, rise." Zontose placed a firm hand on his servant.

"The final hour of the Three Republics is at hand, my lord."

"Indeed it is, Daest, but you did not come before me to point out the obvious. What is it that you want?"

"My kinsmen and I desire to be a part of the ultimate destruction of your foes."

Zontose's eyebrows raised. "Your kinsmen? The osodars are no kin to each other, Daest." Silence ensued for a few moments before Zontose continued speaking. Do you remember, Daest? Do you remember that you are of a different kind than the rest of the osodars?" A thin half smile stretched his lips. "No matter. I am keeping you here for my own plans, and I know the seer will soon provide the services we need. I suppose that doesn't answer your question directly, does it? You need to remain hidden, for if the world knows who I truly am too early, we shall fall into ruin."

"How can that be? In mere days the Republics will be razed to ruin."

"It is something my queen revealed to me, and I have learned to never question her wisdom."

The master led the servant to the far eastern portion of Morhelgol to a chamber with two huge, steel and oak doors barring it. The doors were flanked by four thworfs and two katzians who immediately stiffened upon seeing their masters. Ice instantly formed on the walls and doors before Daest, but the guards pretended not to notice. The katzians heaved the doors inward and immediately closed them after Daest and Zontose passed through.

The chamber was spacious and hexagonal, but one corner arched into a narrower hallway. Red carpet with gold embroideries lined the floor. What few windows were present in the chamber were twelve feet above the ground and blackened. An ubiquitous red glow engulfed the chamber. The air felt cool and dense, and a musty, sulfuric smell permeated it. Deep within the dark corridor, a growl was heard, followed by a shriek and several indecipherable moans. The red glow dimmed somewhat as a voice called out. "Who goes there?" Daest's glowing eyes bore ever toward the darkened hallway, his hand on the pommel of his weapon. He guessed what it was that they had come down here to see, but he didn't trust it. The last time he encountered the creature, it proved to be rather unruly. "I asked who goes there!" the voice growled again.

Click tick, something began to move in the darkness. Click tick, click tick, it sounded again, but faster and faster until at last it emerged: A glossy black creature with green stripes running along its large, bloated body. Six thick, multi-jointed legs propelled the beast along the tile flooring, resembling legs of a spider but more leathery. Its head was like that of a woman but with fanged teeth. Six wings spread out from the body, the tips of each side filling the chamber. The creature's deep sapphire eyes stared at the intruders before she collapsed to the floor. "Forgive me. I did not know it was you," the creature said in a surprisingly pleasant voice.

"Serinah," Zontose whispered.

The creature smiled, dissipated into a deep black mist, and materialized in the shape of a slender woman. She stood taller than the two guests, and she had greenish-gray skin and long red-brown hair. A close-fitting, black, leather dress hung down to the floor.

Serinah walked closer to Zontose, her entire body undulating as she moved serpent-like through the room.

"My lord," she said, bowing her head slightly. "Why have you brought him here?"

"Daest has been loyal to me, and subsequently you, since the beginning. I wanted him to meet my queen."

"I told you I'm not ready yet. My powers are not yet complete. I can hardly maintain a physical form," Serinah hissed.

"You will heed me, Serinah. If I say something, it is so. Have you not learned by now?" growled Zontose.

"Forgive me." Serinah bowed low again. "The osodars are such lowly and pathetic creatures, though. I simply feel you are worthy of much better servants."

"Have you forgotten so much since you last dwelt amongst the living? Do you seriously see yourself as so much higher than them? For you, my dear, dabbled in the secrets of necromancy just like the osodars. The only difference is that you were slain before the ultimate power consumed the rest of us."

"Surely you didn't come here simply to lecture me?" Serinah said.

"I need your counsel. More importantly, I need you to set Daest's mind at ease."

"Meaning?" Serinah said, lowering one eyebrow slightly.

"When will the seer join us? I can feel her doubt, but she will not be persuaded completely. I foresaw just enough to know that the girl would be necessary to bring my plans into fruition, but her obstinance was something

I did not account for. And how long shall we remain hidden?"

"I already told you that if your true name is discovered, it would be your end. You have foes beyond the sea, and in the very heavens themselves, who have yet to strike. As for the girl, it is simply a matter of time and patience. She will soon come around. Why do you ask me questions to which you already know the answer?" Serinah asked.

"Oh, Serinah, you have always had a dramatic touch to you. Of course these are things you already said to me, but I also told you that I wanted Daest to hear it as well."

"There is more, though, isn't there? I can see your mind, and that is not why you brought him here at all."

Zontose let out a boisterous laugh. "My queen, you know me too well!"

"Master, please get on with it. I can hardly retain this form as it is. Pretty soon I will not be able to interact with you at all for some time."

Zontose stepped closer, tucked Serinah's hair behind her ear, and stroked her cheek. "That is why I am here. It is no secret to me how you and the osodars feel about one another, but it was with their help that you came to be on this plane of existence. I am hoping the osodars, particularly Daest, can shed some light on how to bring you back, especially since you were both of the same race."

"That was so long ago, so long …" Daest breathed. "The arts you discovered and taught us affected Serinah and myself differently. I do not see …"

"Precisely!" Zontose interrupted. "You do not see, neither of you do, but it is clear to me. The englifs are a powerful and mysterious people. Neither of you are englifs any longer, but there are still traces of that linage remaining with you, your shapeshifting abilities for one. You, Daest, are so much stronger than the other osodars because of your connection to the englifs."

"What is your plan, my lord?" asked Daest.

"We have only just begun to tap into a power the wizards could not imagine. After the destruction of my original body and my banishment, I delved deeper into it, learning its secrets. How do you think I was able to bring you back to this world?" Zontose paused for a moment, eyeing the others. "The geyser of energy is the key. It is the foundation of the power we discovered. It is no mere coincidence that I founded Dalarashess in this land and build Morhelgol where it stands! The necromancy we discovered is from an era no longer remembered. It syphons energies from the worlox demons that once roamed our world. This is why we could bend our natural talents as wizards to our will. We are no longer slaves to the dogma of Voshnore. We can become gods to the people of Goandria. The power at that well, the Well of Wisdom as I have deemed it, has many secrets, and with it, Serinah, you may have a permanent physical form and help me bring this world to its knees under our will, my will!"

"Is this the truth and joy you promised me, Camalyn?" Raskka inquired, her right knee fidgeting. Her eyes were wide and peering at the floor with the intensity of a cat watching its prey.

"Raskka, you need to calm yourself. You are new here and were out of line to speak in such a way to the prophetess."

"*I* was out of line? You cannot be serious! The goddess wishes us to do good and act with tenderness."

"Raskka, how long will you hold to your child-like notions of the goddess? She is a warrior! We have the divine right to take what we will from the outsiders. All who oppose us oppose the goddess too. You know this, dear. You have had the same upbringing as I, only I have found the Sul to be the source of greater truth. You will as well, Raskka, with time." Camalyn rested a hand on her friend's leg.

A gust of wind blew the deerskin flap on the tent open, sending a cool burst into the shelter. A chill went up Camalyn's spine. "This area is full of the goddesses' power! I can feel her wherever I go. Soon you will be able to as well, Raskka. Don't you see? You only need to spend time under the prophetess' guidance and you will discover the beauty of Hallow Forest. You will have a relationship with her in a way you never knew possible, but you first must be patient and cool that stubborn head of yours."

While Camalyn spoke, Raskka's head remained facing downward. *What have I done? Is this what I have left my family for? I cannot believe this is what the goddess intended when she created us.*

"Raskka!"

"Huh?"

Camalyn threw her hands in the air. "You aren't even listening to me!"

"What if you have been deceived, Camalyn?"

"How do you mean?" Camalyn's eyes narrowed, and Raskka knew she had to choose her words carefully.

"I can't say for sure, but I just feel *off*."

"Your feelings mean very little to me. Of course you are going to feel off. This is new for you. Now hear what I have to say. The prophetess speaks for the goddess. She can be harsh, but it is always for our own good. I have received my fair share of beatings from her, and it served a greater purpose and taught me a great deal."

"To fear her? Camalyn, I chose to leave a fear-based group, and I did not sign up to be part of another one. This is not at all what you said it would be!"

"I said you need to give it time, time enough to see the fruits of your patience. I promise that with just a little bit of patience, a whole new world will open up for you."

"I hope you are right. What brought you here, Camalyn? Why choose to leave the Qunzarria faith for the Sul faction?"

Camalyn shrugged. "I thought that was fairly clear with the conversations we've had."

"Yes, a little, but was it difficult leaving the people we grew up with, the traditions, and the beliefs we held onto so dearly?"

Camalyn ran her fingers along the fur behind her ear a few times before answering. "As I have already said, the prophetess helped me see much more truth than I had ever known before. She has become my spiritual mother, but yes, it was hard at first. It isn't easy giving up something that we were taught as the absolute truth. It became easier to leave when I saw a priestess of the

Qunzarria beating a Sul due to her 'blasphemies' because she was worshipping the goddess somewhere other than the temple. Later, I learned that the priestess had organized raids on the Sul to instill fear and obedience to what she viewed as truth." Camalyn paused. Her throat felt tight, and her eyes reddened. "I soon faced the wrath of the priestess, and it was the prophetess of the Sul that saved me."

"I didn't know ..."

Camalyn waved her hand as if to brush off Raskka's sentiments. "No one does, and it is no longer important. I am not a victim anymore. The frushians are warriors, just as our goddess is. She lets no one else command her, and she does what she wills. I have come to the conclusion that the old Qunzarria have lost their path and chose to only see the goddess through colored glass. Then there is the power." Camalyn flared her fingers, and both her arms soon were alight with crimson flame. "This is only the beginning. The prophetess has shown me it is possible to entirely become living fire."

"But that is not possible!" Raskka gasped.

"Oh, but it is. The magic of the spirits offers so much more than we were taught, and then there is this," Camalyn balled her hands into fists, extinguishing the fire, and then snapped her fingers. Another gust of wind blew open the tent flap again.

"You did that?"

"Yes." Camalyn smirked.

"Before, was that you, too?"

"Haha, no."

"I thought we could only control fire."

"Normally yes, but as I have said already, the prophetess allows you to see things that are normally unseen. You need to give her time."

"Is that something we *should* be doing? The goddess granted us mastery over fire, not any other elements."

"Oh, Raskka, that is what I have been trying to tell you. We have no limits! That was the great lie from our upbringing, that we must worship in a certain place or act in a certain way, but the reality is we can do what we please."

"Is that really how you view the goddess?" Raskka asked, trying to hide her skepticism.

"No, that *is* who the goddess is," Camalyn replied, a thin smile revealing her pointed teeth.

*No, Camalyn, it is not who the goddess is. She is a warrior but also a mother. You once knew that. How could you have forgotten so quickly? What is this mess I have gotten into? Does no one know the goddess anymore? Those men will be put to death, too, just because of some extreme ideology. Then again, the Sul are not the only followers of the goddess that believe we can take what we will from outsiders, but is that right? Is that true? Can we simply take what we want and kill those who defend themselves? I'm so confused, but I know that it is not right to execute them,* Raskka thought.

Mathil and Aron awoke to find themselves tied to the base of a couple tree trunks. Surrounding them was a makeshift barrier of crisscrossed bars about an inch in diameter. There was only six square feet of room within the pen, and the men shared it with a few chickens and ducks. Mathil moaned and shifted in his place continually, but Aron remained still. His eyes were narrowed slightly as they focused on the ground before him. About half an hour passed before Aron's gaze at last shifted toward Mathil. The lower left corner of his lip was between his teeth. Time seemed to slow for Mathil as Aron just stared. Mathil figured the knight to be unhappy, but who wouldn't be in such circumstances? The glowering expression on Aron and his intense gaze made Mathil wonder if perhaps Aron blamed him. Mathil opened his mouth to ask Aron what he was doing, but Aron spoke first. "You had to do it again. Ever since we crossed paths, your mouth has gotten us into trouble!"

Mathil looked around to see if there were any frushians in sight. The thought of one of them ramming a spear or dagger into their hearts for being too loud crossed his mind. "Why are you blaming me, Aron? You were the one that killed their kind, and now they are out for blood, our blood. No, blame me all you want, but this is on you," Mathil retorted in a hushed tone.

"I was protecting you."

"There is more to it, though, isn't there?" Mathil's unblinking eyes locked onto the knight.

"What are you talking about?"

"Can't you see it, Aron? You are angry, always angry, and I hear you when you sleep."

"What difference does it make?" Aron snapped. "We were in danger. These whatever-they-call-themselves attacked us! I am not sorry for defending myself or you."

Mathil shook his head and pursed one side of his mouth together. "You still don't see it. Do I really need to spell it out? I think you enjoyed it, even just a little."

Aron shot daggers at the young man. "What in the world? What sort of accusation is that? I am an archris knight of the Republics. It is my duty to defend others against injustice. Why is it that you can never show any gratitude? A simple thank you would have gone a long way, but no, you simply gripe and blame those around you for your troubles. Maybe, just maybe, instead of passing around blame, you should accept your fate and take it like a man." After Aron finished, he took in several deep breaths, closed his eyes, and clenched his jaw. A final sigh was slowly released from his lungs, and he glanced back at Mathil. "Mathil, I'm sorry. You did not deserve that. You were only speaking your mind, and I got carried away."

Mathil was silent for a few seconds. His eyes moved back to the ground beneath his feet. His heart pumped harder and harder with each moment that went by. Then he looked up. "I understand, Aron. I understand the desire to want to make that animal sitting in Morhelgol pay. This is what I am talking about. You are always tense. I was just hoping you would admit it out loud so you could admit it to yourself."

"I … I do not know what it is. I feel more than just angry. I feel like I continually need to repress my thoughts and feelings, but since …" Aron trailed off. "I just feel aggression waiting to claw its way out, to unleash itself, you know?"

"Aron, you know I have lost people too. You are not alone in Goandria."

Aron couldn't repress the huge grin that formed on his face. "You have driven me nuts ever since we met, but sometimes you speak wisdom, and that is a rare quality in such times."

"Psst!" someone hissed, bringing a quick halt to the conversation.

Neither of the men saw anyone. They strained their ears, but nothing else happened for a few moments. "Psst! Hey, I'm going to get you out of here, but you need to be quiet and still so they don't see you." They both nodded, and then Mathil felt the rope that bound him fall limp. The knife-bearer moved to work on Aron's bonds.

"Now, I need you to get down and crawl on the ground behind the trees. I cut a small opening in the fence for you to sneak through."

Without delay, they did as instructed. Mathil grimaced, hearing squishing noises. He stopped for a moment and saw he was crawling in a minefield of chicken and duck poop.

"What's the matter?" Aron whispered.

"Can you not see what we are crawling in?" Mathil gagged and wrinkled his nose.

"Oh, deal with it. Now's our chance!"

After Aron gave a final push out of the fencing, he saw that the face greeting him was Raskka's. Her brows were furrowed and her eyes narrow as she reached out a furred hand to Aron, pulling him to his feet. She did the same for Mathil and motioned for the two men to keep low. A few yards away, a couple frushians stood deep in conversation.

"I will try to distract them long enough for you to escape."

"Why are you doing this? You will be branded a traitor, and I killed …"

Raskka took Aron's hand. "Because I believe there is more at work here. The goddess has given me a sign and a chance to serve her. I am also coming with you, at least for little while. The Hallow Forest is treacherous. It will play tricks with your mind and get you turned around."

Mathil grimaced but remained quiet. "How do you plan to get us past your people?" Aron asked.

Without a word, spheres of flame manifested in Raskka's palms, she hurled one just past the guards and another further west. Suddenly the camp came alive. Frushians scurried about as the flames leapt higher. The prophetess' voice croaked. "What happened?" she screamed over and over, but the majority of the answers were shrugs or variations of "I don't know." A couple frushians ran to check on the prisoners during the commotion.

"They've escaped!" one shouted, drawing her daggers.

"How could this happen? I secured them myself. There was no way the men could have gotten out of their bonds," the other frushian gasped.

"How indeed," the prophetess said behind the guards-women, causing both to jump.

Both hastily bowed low upon seeing her, then one said, "I swear that we will find them, prophetess."

"Do not be afraid, my children. I know this is not your fault, but it is undeniable that our *guests* had some help. So, by the goddess, you must find them and who is responsible for this betrayal. She will hold you to it," the prophetess said, her tone becoming icy.

Yips and shouts from the frushians echoed all around the escapees. The frushians were like shadows, darting in and out of eyesight, moving so quickly that all Aron and Mathil could see were brownish blurs before a blast of fire was hurled at them. Raskka led the charge, gliding through the forestry with the fluidity of a spirit. In spite of her kin's cunning, she still managed to elude them. The frushians had all spent their entire lives in Hallow, their pursuers even longer than Raskka, yet she had a natural gift of sprinting. In her early years, Raskka prided herself on always being able to outrun her friends. Now she was in a far different race. For the first time, she was fleeing her own people, uncertain of her entire upbringing and the truths she held so dearly. She had left one group for another only to find that things were not always better on the other side. On the outside, Raskka remained composed, stern, and focused, but her spirit and mind were in utter turmoil. She was flooded with a plethora of emotions. She had now betrayed both factions of the Qunzarria faith. *I am an outcast now, with no place to call home. What have I done? Who am I?* Raskka kept asking herself in a continual loop. There was no more certainty for where she was. Everything now rested entirely within the goddess' hands. *Will Qunzarrah ever bring normalcy to my life again? What am I doing with these men? Should I have left them to die? But surely that cannot be the goddess' desire, no matter what Camalyn said. I know the goddess is more than merely a warrior who gives us free reign to do whatever we will. Such a narrow-minded perspective! I wonder what god these men worship, or if they worship one at all. I have heard whispers of a god called Voshnore, but is He any better?*

Moving as swiftly as they possibly could, Aron and Mathil brought up the rear of the trio. Panting as he ran hunched over, Mathil had to hastily duck down further or slide to the ground in order to dodge a few incoming fireballs, one of which nearly singed his hair. Several more explosions of fire erupted around him, and he squatted down for a couple seconds, grateful for the respite from running, but at the same time wishing it was under different circumstances. Confusion momentarily caused Mathil to forget the urgency of his situation, for he peered at the trees the fire hit and saw nothing more than light scorching. *What the? This whole place should be ablaze right now!*

"Mathil! What are you doing? Come on!" Aron cried out, jarring him back to reality. Over small hills and through vine infestations, they sprinted, never looking back. None of them knew when exactly the attacks stopped. Eventually, the frushians were no longer seen out of the corners of their eyes, nor were their calls heard. Mathil and Aron nearly collapsed from fatigue when they rested.

"Do you think we lost them?" Mathil asked between breaths.

"Oh no, they will be out looking for us, and they will find us if we linger in the forest too long. They may be watching us right now. Remember, we can fly, and you can't. It is not easy to hide from a frushian long, especially in the Hallow Forest. We are one with Hallow. What the forest feels, we feel. There are those, of course, who are more sensitive than others."

"How much longer until we reach the border?" voiced Aron.

131

"Little less than ten miles, but on foot it will take time, time that we do not have. Rest and eat while you can, boys. We will need to get moving shortly, and we won't be able to stop until we reach the end."

Mathil shuddered at the thought of even more time in Hallow Forest. He wrapped his arms around his knees and buried his face, attempting to conceal his terror. *I couldn't sleep here anyway*, he thought. His mind once again revisited the haunting experiences from two nights ago. Mathil knew what happened to him was not his imagination, no matter what Aron might have said about the ordeal. The young man looked at the knight. *Always the skeptic. I wonder if his "rational" reasoning sounds as absurd to him when he says it out loud as it does to me. I wonder how he cannot feel the creepy vibe this place gives off*, he thought. Mathil then noticed that Raskka was pacing back and forth like a caged animal while he and Aron sat. *I wonder how Aron feels about her tagging along with us. I really doubt she is truly doing all this out of the kindness of her heart. None of this makes any sense. This whole place doesn't make sense.*

They each ate a few berries that were close, and Raskka allowed the men twenty minutes of rest before she pushed them onward once again. Mathil's lungs felt like fire in his chest, and his legs burned in agony, yet he knew the truth of what Raskka said. He could not stop, though his body begged him for some respite. To Mathil, the knight did not appear to be phased by the prolonged run through the forest, and Raskka was even less troubled. The dainty frushian scampered along the forest floor without any panting or signs of being hindered by the density of the woodland.

The night at last began to wane, and dim rays of light glinted off the gold and violet leaves above. The forest's eerie glow began to return, and with it, a blanket of fog rolled in from the northwest. At first the fog's density was thin, and the three companions managed to keep moving swiftly, but after nearly an hour had passed, the situation quickly changed.

"What is with this place and fog?" Mathil grumbled.

"It isn't fog," Raskka said as her eyes narrowed, and she pursed her lips together. "At least not the fog of the world."

"Don't tell me you are going to tell him more ghost stories. The poor guy is already scared of this place. There is no need to fill his head with more nonsense," Aron cut in.

"What do you mean?" Mathil asked defensively.

"Ever since we arrived, you haven't been sleeping. That wonderful camp we were in doesn't count. You rarely blink, and when you get more than a moment of rest, you start trembling. You aren't very good at hiding your fear, Mathil. I think you scared yourself with those ghost stories you told me about."

"How can you be such a skeptic? You have seen things, strange things, and even spiritual things! You have told me stories," Mathil countered.

"Because I know such things are an exception and not the norm of the world."

"What makes you say that?" Raskka asked. "Is it possible you do not understand as much of the world as you may think?"

Aron was silent. His expression was blank, save for a slight tightening of his brows.

"You may have had many travels across Goandria and experienced many things, but there is much you have yet to learn," Raskka said.

"Don't lecture me, Raskka. My … I once knew someone with strong ties to the spiritual realm. She had a great power and was murdered for it. I have also experienced much more than I wish to share, so do not presume to imply that my heart is hardened."

Raskka raised her hands. "I meant no offense. I was merely trying to offer another perspective on the matter. I do not think you should throw away Mathil's concerns so readily. There are things in this forest that would challenge your presuppositions."

# Chapter 9

With several miles now behind them, the Hallow Forest began to thin, and the fields of Verntail were distantly visible. The sky held large, puffy, clouds and the sun occasionally smiled down upon them, reminding the company that their trek through the forest was nearly over. A mild breeze combed through the landscape, wafting with it smells of flowers and grasses just beyond the woodland.

Mathil's heart leapt at seeing the end of the forest, but then it quickly sank. Across the sky a half-dozen fiery blazes leapt into view and then vanished. "The frushians. They tracked us down."

"Of course they did. We are mistresses of the forest. It was only a matter of time before they found us," replied Raskka. As the words left Raskka's lips, another handful of frushians flew across the sky. "Stay down!" she whispered. Then a burst of bright red flame shot past her head as she ducked to the side.

"Raskka! Raskka! We know you are here. We can smell you. If you give yourself up, the prophetess will show you mercy," Camalyn's voice echoed.

Aron looked at Raskka. His own expression revealed nothing as he stared at her. "What are you doing?" Mathil's hushed voice suddenly asked, shattering his train of thought.

"Huh?"

"You are staring holes through her. What are you doing?"

"Why?" Aron whispered.

"Why? Because it's creepy. You are going to give the poor woman a complex."

"No, I mean why do you have to know everything and ask the stupidest questions?"

"Wow, someone's in a bad mood."

"I'm curious about something," said Aron.

"You want to know if she will betray us to her sisters," Mathil asked matter-of-factly.

"Of course I do."

"Hasn't she proven that she is our friend? She risked so much."

"Maybe *your* friend," Aron replied.

"You don't trust anyone, do you?" Mathil shook his head.

"If you lived through what I have, you wouldn't either. Did I ever tell you that I once knew the monster who calls himself Zontose? I knew him when he was an archris knight like me. I not only knew him, but trusted and loved him. Now everything I have ever loved is destroyed. That is what trust gets you in this world, Mathil."

Before Mathil could answer, Raskka rolled over to them. "You two are whispering so loudly, it's a wonder they haven't found us yet! What is so important that you two must talk about it right now?"

"Raskka, come out!" Camalyn shouted once again. "We are your sisters. I know you don't understand, but the prophetess is not your enemy unless you continue to rebel against her and the goddess."

A clawed hand stretched from behind a tree, grasping Raskka's shoulder. "Got you!" As she was dragged to her feet, suddenly all grew dim. Echoes of voices became intertwined with the howl of the wind. All color seemed to be sapped from the world, and Raskka grew very dizzy. The face of the frushian before her flashed in her mind, but images of black shades darting back and forth consumed her consciousness.

"What ... what's ..." she struggled to say.

"What's the matter, Raskka?" the frushian asked, but Raskka continued to stare off beyond the other woman, her eyes unblinking. Then, as quickly as it all began, the sun shone through once again, and the vibrant colors of the world greeted her once more before she was punched in the gut. "Did you really think your treachery would go unnoticed, Raskka?"

"I would rather betray a self-proclaimed prophetess than the goddess herself, Lindael," Raskka gasped. She hurled her own fists into Lindael. Before the other frushian knew what hit her, Raskka withdrew one of her daggers and stabbed the other in the chest.

"I will not be intimidated by anyone," she whispered in Lindael's ear as she lowered the body to the ground.

"Has it really come down to this?"

Raskka whirled around to see Camalyn with her arms folded across her chest. Camalyn's eyes narrowed as she glared at her former friend. "You would choose outsiders over your sisters? *Men* over us?"

"I was a fool, Camalyn. I let our friendship stand in the way of truth. The Sul are not persecuted! The Sul are not the innocent Qunzarria. Neither faction is! One side fanatically decrees that we must only worship in the temple, and the other follows a heretic. Your prophetess has set herself up in a place of power. You are ruled by her, not by the goddess."

"How dare you speak such blasphemies!" snarled Camalyn. "I was hoping that you would have come to your senses by the time I caught up to you, but clearly those males infected you far deeper than I imagined. I shall relish bringing your head to the prophetess."

"You will try," Aron said, unsheathing his sword with Mathil beside him.

"Aw, look, your man-friends come to your rescue, Raskka," Camalyn jeered. The rest of the frushians emerged from the woods, their daggers drawn as they encircled the trio.

"You sanctimonious fools! How do you think this is going to end for you? You kill us, and then what? You will never be free. You are slaves to your almighty prophetess," said Raskka.

"I have heard enough out of you. Kill them," Camalyn commanded. The frushians quickly moved in, their daggers whirling before them.

"Stay behind me," Aron said to Mathil.

"Don't worry. I don't think I am ready to put your lessons to the test quite yet."

Three lunged at Aron, and he quickly parried their blows and dispatched them, but four more quickly took their fallen comrades' places. Raskka dashed in to aid Aron. She countered a series of dagger attacks before delivering a spinning kick to one of her sisters and stabbing another. More and more frushians moved in. Raskka and Aron stood back to back as Mathil attempted to duck behind a fallen tree. "Great, I'm going to let Raskka and Aron fight for me as I hide ..." he said to himself. "No, I'm not going to be a coward!" As soon as he stuck his head out from behind the trunk, a frushian screamed and swung a dagger at him.

All around, the frushians swarmed in from their hiding places. Raskka's weapons whirled unceasingly, but at last her weapons were knocked from her hands. "There are too many!" she called back to Aron. Her palms ignited in a bright red flame, and fiery wings burst from her back. Her eyes glistened, and her lips pursed together. In that moment, she seemed to grow larger, into a terrible spirit of vengeance, and the frushians briefly halted their assault. Aron dared not to breathe, for all was silent. Not even a bird or the whistle of the wind could be heard. The sounds of life flooded back into the wilderness, and a blinding flash of fire shot forth from Raskka's hands, incinerating a dozen frushians.

Murmurs instantly rose up amongst the women. Many backed off or dropped their weapons and fled into the forest. "Run!" Raskka shouted to the men. Without hesitation, they did as she said. Raskka trailed behind as they ran full speed through the remains of the forest. When the sea of trees finally gave way to the prairie lands of Verntail, they stopped. Mathil doubled over, clenching his chest as he tried to catch his breath. Aron looked back at the forest. There was no sign of the frushians. The fresh, crisp air of Verntail filled his lungs. When the knight reopened his eyes, his heart sank. A score or more of fiery wings beat toward them.

"It looks like we aren't done with your friends yet, Raskka," Aron said, pointing to the sky.

"Do you hear something?" Raskka asked suddenly.

"Yes, death. Aron already said the frushians are coming!" Mathil snapped as the frushians encircled them once again.

"No, I hear tromping far off. What is that?" Raskka said again.

Mathil drew his weapon. "I think she's lost it, Aron."

However it wasn't just Raskka that seemed distracted. As the other women withdrew their weapons, they looked around. Each pair of eyes darted madly, trying to uncover the secret behind the far off din.

Aron took his chance. His sword tip swung unhindered at his foe. Before the blade struck, his prey instantly rose to the challenge, and Aron's blow was met with an unrelenting assault of her daggers. The frushians came alive, their daggers moving in to deliver a final blow to the traitor and her new companions. Then something caught Mathil's ear. "Aron! Do you hear *horses*?"

"I'm a little busy right now," he called back through the clanging of steel.

The frushians halted again as the sound drew nearer. Everyone's eyes again scoured the land. Two dozen horsemen were seen galloping over the hilltop. One of the cavaliers shot an arrow in the midst of the frushians, causing them to scatter. Most fled back into the forest, but a couple extended their wings and took to the sky. "How dare they fire upon the sacred people of the goddess!" one exclaimed as she hurled a ball of fire at the riders. A few of the soldiers were incinerated by the blast, which resulted in the frushian being peppered with arrows. That was the last straw for those who had previously resolved to stand and fight, and when the horsemen arrived, all that remained were Raskka, Mathil, and Aron.

The horse riders stopped before the trio. "This is an unexpected pleasure!" Aron announced as an arrow struck the ground at his feet.

"Who are you, why are you trespassing, and why did you attack us?" an older soldier with a gold rimmed helm inquired.

Stepping back, Aron's eyes locked onto the soldier's. "I am an archris knight of the Three Republics sent on a mission from the High King himself to see if anyone survived the decimation of Grivear City. This young man was the only one still alive when I arrived, and this is Raskka. She freed us from those who attacked you. Due to her help, we were pursued by her people, the frushians, and they attacked you."

"Not to mention you kinda shot first," Mathil mumbled.

"Quiet!" Aron snapped.

The soldier's eyes narrowed. "Well then, luck is indeed on your side. If what you say is true, it can be easily verified by the king. He is in Belthora as we speak."

"Don't worry about it. I don't think they are anything to worry about," another voice added.

Aron's heart leapt. "Quartose, is that you?"

"Aron!" Quartose exclaimed, embracing the other knight. "Where have you been?"

"You know him?" the mounted soldier inquired, raising a single eyebrow.

"He is the hardiest archris knight in the entire army, sergeant. Not to mention the greatest man I have ever known. He and I were stationed at the Grivear Academy when the war first broke out. Then …"

"We parted ways for a time," Aron cut in. "I mostly did recon for King Ivo, which as I stated before, is how I came across these two."

"Well, if Quartose trusts you, I don't have a problem. Now it's time we get moving. The thworfs will be upon the city within a day or two at most," the sergeant said.

"Wait, what are you talking about?" Aron interrupted.

"Zontose has sent an invasion force to eliminate the final strongholds of the Republics. We were on patrol when we found you," said Quartose.

"Why don't you escort your friend back to Belthora, and we will continue scouting?" suggested the sergeant.

"Alright, but be careful out there." Quartose nodded.

"San and Emmor will accompany you so your friends can ride to the city." Then the sergeant turned to Aron. "But be warned, if you go into the city, it is unlikely that you will be able to leave before the battle is upon you."

"Battle?" Mathil's voice cracked.

"Safety is not guaranteed for any of you. If you do not know how to fight or do not wish to fight, I would suggest you turn back now."

"If it means finally getting the chance to push back against Zontose, I'm in. I'm not completely useless in battle. Aron showed me a few tricks, and I have some experience with a sword."

142

"It will be far different than the few times you had to defend yourself, Mathil," Aron retorted. "Besides, I do not remember giving you any lessons . . ."

Mathil just gave a half smirk in response.

"I think this is where we shall depart, my friends. I aided you as long as I could, but I have no interest in fighting in men's wars. Good luck, and may the goddess protect you." Raskka embraced Aron and Mathil. "It was a pleasure meeting such honorable men for once."

"If you need anything, do not hesitate to ask," Aron said. With a smile, Raskka took to the sky, leaving the others speechless.

"Ugh, I don't think I can ever get used to riding," Mathil moaned.

"San gave up his steed so that we can ride, so maybe you should show some gratitude. You know, it seems you need to be reminded to be grateful rather often," Aron remarked.

The soldiers did not seem to pay any mind to the knight and Mathil during the exchange. Their expressions remained unchanged and their gazes rarely wavered from their focus. Quartose, however, could not help himself. He continually stared at the two, privately wondering what sort of relationship Aron and Mathil had. *Are they friends? They don't act like friends. Maybe something else binds them together. I wonder why Mathil is even here. He doesn't seem to be happy traveling with us, in spite of his grand claims of wanting to fight Zontose. Not to mention he admitted to being an amateur with a sword. I wonder what Aron's goal is with this young man. Maybe he feels responsible for him as someone he can look after since the loss of his family,* Quartose thought as his gaze remained on them.

"What do you think of the frushians?" Mathil asked. "I mean, Raskka was nice, but their religion is something I have never heard of before. I met a few people who didn't believe in Voshnore, but no one who worshipped a completely different deity. What do you think? Do you think there are other deities?"

Aron was silent for a bit before he answered. Turning his head slightly to the left, he said, "There are definitely many things we cannot explain in the world. I do not know much about the frushians or their faith other than our recent experiences, but I can say with certainty that Voshnore is real. I have experienced His miracles, I have seen His servants, and I once knew someone very dear to me who was a seer."

"A seer?"

"Someone who has the ability to see into the spiritual realm. Sometimes the past, distant lands, or even future events are revealed to them," Aron answered.

"Wow, you knew someone like that? What are these other things you experienced?" Mathil pressed.

"I would rather not talk about it."

Mathil cocked his head and raised one eyebrow slightly. "That's just like you. Whenever our conversation takes a turn to your past, you suddenly get so mysterious about it and close me out."

"It's my business, and my story to tell when I am ready."

"Fine, have it your way." Mathil waved it off. "Where do you think the frushians' magic comes from?

The wizards' power is a gift from Voshnore, but they do not worship him," Mathil said.

"Zontose has magic, and he sees himself as a god. There are obviously things in the system that we do not understand. I do not think all magic is the same; maybe dark powers grant it, or maybe it is something else entirely."

"The frushians are just so different. It made me rethink things that I thought I knew to be true. I thought all of Goandria, save for the non-believers and the thworfs who worship Zontose, followed Voshnore."

Aron smiled. "Then this is one of many lessons to take away from this. We should never assume what the world believes. It will often get us into trouble, but everyone is guilty of it."

"What did you make of them?" Mathil asked.

"They are an angry race of women. I wondered what they did with their men. I kept envisioning a group of frushian men holed up in the ground somewhere, hiding from their scary wives," Aron smirked. "But if you are referring to their religion, I don't know. As an archris knight, I have seen many things. There is a wide-array of beliefs in Goandria, but that does not make what we believe any less real or the lessons we can learn any less important. There may be several interpretations to reality, but that does not negate the fact that there is only one ultimate reality."

"I guess you are right." Mathil slowly nodded.

Within the gates, the air was warmer and filled with the aroma of the city gardens. Aron took in a deep breath. "Belthora, the city of wonder and beauty. You know, Mathil, I always thought this should have been the Capital of the Republics instead of Hondor. It is so much more vibrant in every way." Then he turned to Quartose. "Is this where you have been all this time?"

"Well, not the *whole* time." Quartose winked.

"This is pure luxury, especially compared to where we have been." Mathil's eyes were wide, taking in the sights around him.

"San, Emmor, you are dismissed," Quartose said. "Now to speak with our High King and the senate." He sighed.

"Hey, after our trek through Hallow Forest, a boring day with politicians is very welcome," Mathil remarked.

"Aron, I think your friend should be careful what he wishes for," said Quartose.

"Indeed, but ignorance abounds with this young man, so you shouldn't expect any more."

"Hey, I'm right here!" Mathil shireked.

"Hmm, I see what you mean," Quartose remarked with a half-smile forming on his lips.

"Yeah, haha, very funny guys."

Quartose led them to the courtyard before Belthora's palace. Amongst the statues stood a corpulent figure gawking at one of these statues. A crown sat cockeyed upon his massive head, which slowly turned toward the newcomers. His inset eyes gleamed in the sunlight. He raised a hand and called out, "Aron! They told me you were coming. It is so good to see you."

"Likewise, your majesty."

Ivo shuffled along the ground to meet the knights and Mathil. "I was beginning to wonder if you were ever

146

going to return from your mission. I regretted ever sending you in the first place. I figured that place was a graveyard, but I had to know if anyone survived or if the rumors were indeed true. What took you so long?"

Aron placed his hand on Mathil's shoulder. "This was the only survivor I found in that ruined city. The rumors you heard were true. And to answer your question would take far too much time. Ultimately, there was a lot that stood in our way of returning."

"It was maybe a week or two after you left that I learned the truth of Grivear City. I was praying you would return."

"Your highness!" a voice suddenly screamed out. Ivo turned, seeing the sergeant Aron and Mathil encountered earlier riding toward him. "Zontose's armies. They knew we were coming somehow. I am the only one that survived. They are a lot closer than our last reports stated. They will be upon the city within hours!"

"Hours? That is just perfect! How is it possible our scouts could have been so wrong?" The king raged, turning his back. "Zontose planned this all along. Someone else is feeding him information," he murmured to himself. "We must prepare the city. Send word to the captains that Zontose's forces will be here soon. Send messengers to Hondor as well. They will be blindsided by an attack this early if we do not warn them."

Aron stepped forward. "Mathil and I will go to Hondor. We will deliver your message and help defend the city in any way we can."

"But you've only just arrived, and you've been through so much already. I couldn't possibly ask you to …"

"It is my duty, your majesty," Aron cut in.

"And I want to see that monster get what's coming to him for invading our lands," Mathil added.

# Chapter 10

None knew how long the archers along the wall waited. Two hundred bowmen lined the outer wall, their eyes steely and expressions stern. Few words were exchanged amongst them. Their glistening armor blazed in the twilight, and helms concealed their expressions from their comrades. Quartose ceaselessly paced back and forth above the gate, ever keeping an eye on the grasslands beyond. The wind combed through the tall grasses, and large, puffy clouds filled the sky. Birds sang, and animals frolicked through the fields, but Quartose knew it was all an illusion. His eyes caught something in a distance. The knight paused, tilting his head slightly. The nearby bowmen tensed their hands around their weapons. However, whatever it was darted off. Quartose continually told himself it was just another animal, but his focus remained, though nothing showed itself.

A knight suddenly appeared behind him. "Sir, we await your command," he announced.

Quartose jumped, his hand immediately grasping the hilt of his weapon. "Lieutenant, never do that again!"

"Sir?" the bewildered soldier asked.

"Sorry, never mind. I'm just a bit on edge. Have the cavalry ready at the gate, and reinforce the walls. Bring nine-hundred archris knights to the walls. We will need more than archers up here. See to it that the kings and queen are well guarded and that we have archers posted on the higher-levels in case the enemy breaks through. Also make sure we have reserves stationed in the marketplace. That will be the first point of entry if the gate is broken."

"Right away, sir. Anything else?"

Before Quartose could answer, the bellowing of horns echoed across the plain. He pivoted on one heel to face the oncoming army. Dozens of black dragons flew above amidst the backdrop of the pale setting sun. On the ground, thousands upon thousands of thworfs marched in formation with giant katzians at the head of each battalion. Drums boomed louder and louder as the army advanced. Never before had the people of Belthora seen such a staggering force. The din of steel boots and clanking metal filled the air. When the army finally halted before the wall, the thworfs began singing.

Quartose leaned in closer to the wall. His face tightened, but he still could not make out the words of the thworf song. Some raised their swords and shouted out what appeared to be insults, some simply stood at attention, and others thumbed their weapons, itching for the battle to start. As the thworfs continued singing, two large masses of cavalry flanked either side of the army.

Quartose's eyes widened. "How could they," he breathed, for the horsemen were not thworfs at all. They were humans clad in fur and leather. One of the horsemen rode toward the gate bearing a white flag.

"What do you suppose they are getting at? Zontose has never offered a chance to discuss terms before," an archer said to Quartose.

"No, no, he hasn't. They are toying with us."

"What shall we do then?"

"I will ride out and see what he has to say. If there is a chance to avoid bloodshed, no matter how small, we must take it. Besides, I'm very curious to hear what he has to say." Quartose smirked.

Quartose mounted his horse, and the gate opened just enough for him to pass through before it thudded shut again. The man holding the white flag was tall, and a slender, red-brown beard engulfed his face. A long sword and bow were strapped to his back. His face was emotionless save for his eyes that looked coldly at Quartose. For a few seconds, they stared silently, unwaveringly at one another, but the seconds felt like hours to Quartose.

"I take it you have something to say, so just say it," Quartose said at last.

"Indeed, I do," the northman's voice boomed like thunder. "As you can see, our forces are far larger than your own. Lord Zontose, in his wisdom and mercy, allows you this one chance to surrender all archris knights and remaining soldiers to him. If you comply, the civilians will be allowed to live."

"For what price did he buy you? What amount was enough to betray your own kind?" Quartose snarled.

"What is your answer? Will you surrender yourself and the armies of the Republics to Zontose so that your people may survive?"

"When has Zontose ever demonstrated any sort of sincerity or given us any reason to trust his intentions now? Will the knights and soldiers of the Republics surrender so that our people may live in oppression under a tyrant who considers himself a god? Never."

"You dare reject Zontose's kindness? Who are you but a mere archris knight? Where is the king? Perhaps Ivo has more reason than you."

"Your people and the king's collaborations have done enough damage." Quartose spurred his steed back inside Belthora, leaving the other speechless.

When he returned to the wall, Quartose called out, "Zontose demands that we surrender ourselves so that the citizens of the Republics are allowed to live, but how can we abandon our people to such a cruel fate? How can we allow Zontose to rule Goandria unchecked? Is that what so many of our archris knights and soldiers gave their lives for? No! Prepare yourselves, for the thworfs will show no mercy. Be ready because not all of you will live through the night. We fight for the lives of our people, our parents, our brothers, our sisters, and our friends. We fight so that we may one day see Goandria free from this evil!"

The soldiers cheered, beating their fists and swords against their breastplates and shields. In that moment, the thworf army moved in. The men of Dalarashess notched arrows to their bows and loosed a volley over the walls of the city. The thworf infantry hauled up wooden siege ladders as their human allies continued to launch barrage after barrage of arrows upon the defenders.

"Return fire at will. Do not let up!" Quartose cried out over the din of the ensuing battle. Archer after archer was picked off by the longbows of Dalarashess. *Clank, clank* the siege ladders sounded as they were raised. Thworfs by the dozens began to clamber up to the top of the walls. Gray and brown feathered arrows pelted the thworfs, but still more came.

"We need reinforcements!" Quartose shouted over his shoulder, unsure if anyone was around to hear him. He slashed at a couple thworfs that had reached the top.

As the thworfs attacked the wall head-on, the katzians lugged trebuchets closer to the city. There was a score of them, each with stone wheels twice the height of a thworf, and each frame stood three times taller than any katzian. The boulder projectiles were heaved into position by two katzians each. Once in the sling, the large rocks were smothered in oil and set aflame.

"Loose the trebuchets!" ordered the thworf general. The siege engines moaned as they tossed their payload.

Upon the wall, Quartose's eyes widened. "Take cover!" he yelled out just before the huge rocks smote the wall. *Thud, thud.* They crashed on top of the wall, into the wall's face, and even into some of the buildings closest to the wall. Each time the stones struck, shockwaves were sent through the city. Dozens of archers were instantly killed, and the wall itself splintered where it was hit. Some of the soldiers who were not hit by the initial impact were set ablaze, fragments of rock lay strewn about the outer portion of the city, and clouds of dust choked the lungs of the defenders.

Again the trebuchets unleashed a barrage of boulders at the wall, and this time the center began to crumble inward, crushing soldiers from both armies. Quartose was hurled backward and landed face down on a broken wall piece. Most of the archers and archris knights near him were not so lucky. Coughing viciously, Quartose attempted to lift himself up, but his arms gave way. After several minutes, he finally managed to roll over. He cradled his head as his vision blurred. Blood trickled down his forehead and into his eyes. Above him, he caught glimpses of thworfs. Quartose wiped his eyes with his tunic. Lifting his head slightly, he saw the enemy had overrun his position. He could not quite see how much of the wall had been taken, but the knight guessed things were not going well.

Black dragons soared into the city. Their thworf riders hopped off, joining their fellow attackers in the city. The steeds flew to the inner city, unleashing a fiery torrent upon the people. Women scurried, attempting to douse the flames, but the dragons relentlessly scorched all in their path. Plumes of smoke billowed into the sky. Archers perched upon the higher levels of the city ceaselessly plucked their bowstrings, but none could hit the dragons.

*Crash, crash,* another round of boulders slammed into the wall, completely crumbling the midsection. Thworfs, men of Dalarashess, and katzians all pressed through the wall unhindered. The mounted archris knights rode toward the damaged wall, and hundreds of spears met the relentless flow of enemies. Quartose mustered all the strength he had and rushed to the destroyed section of the wall.

"Do not let them through! Push on!" he screamed before doubling over again, clenching his side. He figured at least a couple ribs were broken, and perhaps even more damage had been done, but he could not think of that now.

"Sir, we need reinforcements!" a knight exclaimed as his spear thrust through a thworf's head.

"Keep fighting! Remember what you are fighting for!" Quartose cheered on. His face bore a smile as he spoke, and he tried to make his voice uplifting, but he saw that the odds were against them. Before him, the massive strength of Zontose's armies were revealed in all their might. It did not seem to matter how many were killed. There were many more to replace the fallen. In the space where the wall had crumbled, thworf bodies continued to pile up so high that Zontose's army needed to climb over their dead only to be struck down before they reached their prey.

"Maybe there is hope after all," Quartose uttered under his breath. Six katzians thundered over to the archris knights. Two katzians started clearing the thworf and knight corpses from the gap in the wall. Unsheathing their massive weapons, the rest of the katzians came down upon the knights. The large swords struck down two or three archris knights and their horses at once. In a matter of minutes, half of the archris knights were killed. "Pull back!" Quartose commanded. As the knights turned to flee further into the city, the thworfs and katzians struck down several more.

With two battering rams, the thworfs easily smashed through the unguarded gate. Soon thworfs and katzians were everywhere within the city, and black dragons continued to rain fire down upon Belthora. Within the city palace, King Locke, his wife, and King Ivo watched as the fires grew closer and closer to them. Ash collected on the statues and gardens of the palace, and the crystal waters that gave life to the city ran black.

"The city is lost, Locke," Ivo stated rather matter-of-factly.

"Not yet. We still have men defending Belthora," Locke responded quietly.

"We must leave while we can. We are no good to the Republics dead!" Ivo urged.

"And we are no good to our people if we are cowards, Ivo. If you wish to leave, do so, but I have hidden long enough." Withdrawing his sword, he turned to the royal guards. "It is time we help the others. Send word to the reinforcements that we will push forward immediately."

"Locke, that is suicide!" the queen protested.

"You cannot go out there. I will not allow it!" Ivo demanded.

"Your rule is no longer recognized in my city or in Verntail, you coward!" Locke snapped. "It is your actions that contributed to this mess, and I am done making excuses for you."

"How dare you! I am your king, the High King of the Three Republics!" Ivo exploded.

"You are nothing but a fat man trying to grasp for power that isn't and never was yours." Locke led his soldiers out of the palace.

Two horses galloped across the grassy plains, carrying Mathil and Aron at full speed from Belthora to Hondor. A shadow flickered in the corner of Mathil's eye, and he instinctively glanced behind him. "Aron! Aron!" he gasped, hoping the knight heard him over the galloping of hooves. He called out again, and Aron drew in the reins of his steed. Black and gray smoke billowed into the air from Belthora. Little black dots bearing lights surrounded the city as fire balls continued to pummel the stone. Jets of fire endlessly poured from dragons swarming the city from above.

So many emotions hit Aron as he sat upon his restless steed. His eyes saw the terror of Belthora, but his heart could not believe it. The great city he once knew was being destroyed from all sides. His eyes turned red, and tears streamed down his cheeks onto his cloak. Aron wanted to say something, but no words formed upon his lips. *The terror those people must feel, the uncertainty ...* he thought as flames of the waning light danced in his eyes.

"We must keep moving," he finally said. "Otherwise Hondor will suffer the same fate."

Mathil turned to the knight, his face red and puffy and his cheeks soaked. "What is the point? Who can stop all this?"

"I don't know," admitted Aron. "But we can warn Hondor, and maybe they will have a fighting chance."

As the horses stormed off toward Ashear's capital, no words were exchanged between the two. Mathil continually wondered who was still alive, if any at all. *Would one man survive the siege of the city, like I was the sole survivor of Grivear City? I wonder if Belthora or Grivear City will be rebuilt someday. Probably not. With the size of that army coming through, it is doubtful any of the cities will remain. I guess we all wanted an end to this war, and that is exactly what is coming,* he thought.

Eventually the blackness of night engulfed the world, and all that Aron could see of Belthora was the dim flicker of flames. "Oh, Voshnore, why has it come to this? Why does Zontose always seem a step ahead of us? Is he fated to conquer Goandria?" the knight prayed silently. So many emotions filled him; dread, fear, anxiety, and despair bombarded him. His brown eyes shifted to the sky. "I need You, and I need Your guidance. You have made Yourself known in the past, but You seem so far away. Lord Voshnore, I lost my beautiful wife, my special girl, and so many are losing even more to this monster. What does it take to stop him? What is Your plan for all of this? Do You even have a plan? Are You even listening?" After the last question, he stopped, letting the wind sift through his long, scraggly hair. He took a deep breath and then exhaled. Just then, a loud swoosh abruptly caught his attention.

The sound seemed rather distant, but Aron had a hard time telling exactly how far away it was due to the wind rushing in his ears. He saw the flames of Belthora behind him. "I must be hearing things. It is probably just the combination of the wind and the horses galloping," Aron said under his breath. Then he saw two red-orange wings glowing amidst the night sky. "That is definitely not dragon fire."

"Huh?" Mathil perked up, but before he could say any more, the winged creature was upon them.

"Looks like things are not going well for you either," a female voice said.

"Raskka!" Mathil cried out. "What are you doing here?"

"I thought you decided to leave," Aron added.

"Well, the last thing I want to do is get caught up in someone else's war, but I cannot go home for the time being. The Sul are still searching for me, and I don't want to put my community in jeopardy, so here I am."

"Your timing is impeccable. We are on our way to Hondor to warn them of the impending invasion. Just so we are clear, are you here to fight as well?"

"Right to the point, Aron." Raskka chuckled. "Yes, I will fight with you. I figure it is only a matter of time before my people are caught up in this war too."

"And you have nowhere else to go," Mathil said.

"Perhaps, perhaps not. It is whatever the goddess desires. I feel things are changing, and I would be a fool to ignore them."

"Things have been *changing* for a while now, Raskka," Aron said.

"For you, perhaps. The world is much larger than the Three Republics, and perhaps there are more places in Goandria that Zontose cannot reach."

"Perhaps …" Aron said more to himself than to the frushian. "If you are coming, that is fine, but we really must be going. Time is short." The knight spurred his horse, and Mathil silently followed. Raskka flew above them for a while. Mathil watched her gracefully glide through the air, the wind sifting through her blonde locks. Her armor gleamed slightly in the starlight, catching the young man's eye every time he turned away. Raskka was unlike anyone he had seen before, and he found her exotic beauty beyond comparison.

The frushian caught Mathil staring at her, and she quickly turned away, a thin smile spreading across her lips. She folded her wings inward, dove down, then at the last moment her wings unfolded, stopping her midair as she leapt onto back of the saddle behind Mathil. "You look like there is something on your mind."

"Uh … me?" Mathil asked, rather dumbfounded.

"If you have something to say, just say it," Raskka prodded gently.

"You, your culture, and your people are all so new to me," Mathil said slowly, glancing shyly at her.

"And I haven't come across many humans, especially men, in my life."

"I would like to know more about your people, your ways, and your religion. I never knew any of this existed before."

Raskka chuckled. "You ask questions that have very long answers."

"I guess I like to learn new things," Mathil said.

"Well, to tell you the history of my people would take too much time right now, and there are more pressing matters, but while we are traveling, I can tell you about our beliefs. So you do not know about the goddess, Qunzarrah, or her mate, Uron?"

Mathil shook his head, and Raskka continued. "Qunzarrah is the mistress of all, and she is the most worthy of all the gods and goddesses. She is the goddess of strength, power, and wisdom. She is a warrior who claimed the heavens as her own through strength. She bent all the spirits and gods to her will, including her husband who was once the lord of all. For Uron, the god of which I speak, is a timid fool who cowers at the thought of confrontation. If only you could have seen her, Mathil. The majesty of her appearance! Her ebony skin, bulging muscles, orange-yellow eyes, and green hair. She is a marvel to behold!"

"You have actually *seen* this goddess?" Mathil asked, and although Raskka could not see it, Mathil's eyes narrowed, and his brows hung low.

"Well yes, of course! All frushians have. We are her chosen people. Haven't you seen your god?"

"Well, I have seen His hand in my life, but I cannot say I have physically seen Him, so no."

"And still you believe? How do you know that He listens to you, or even exists?"

"It is the little things in life, such as me surviving when everyone else in my city was killed. I take it as a sign. I have also felt His love and presence which transcends all description. Not to mention I have known people, including Aron here, who have experienced the Sala and other messengers of Voshnore. What about you? Have you ever felt the presence of your goddess' love?"

"Hmm, not in the same way you describe," Raskka said slowly. "Our goddess is power to us, and we revere her for that. She is the embodiment of strength in the world, and she shows how the woman was always meant to dominate the man."

Mathil rolled his eyes. *She talks about men like they are some foreign concept and like she does not even realize I am one of them,* he thought.

After some time, Raskka unfurled her wings and rocketed into the air without saying a word. Nearly an hour passed before Raskka's voice abruptly blurted, "I see a settlement!"

"Yes, we are almost there. Let us hope there is enough distance between us and the thworfs to give the city ample warning," said Aron.

A wide mass of dark lumber rose up, supported by steel beams and large nails with heads two-inches in diameter. A square gate comprised of double doors sat in the center, and scores of armored sentries bearing spears and bows lined the top.

"Halt! Who goes there?" one of the sentries yelled out from the wall. Upon seeing Raskka, the archers aimed their bows at her. Most seemed more concerned with her than with the men on horseback.

"I'm Aron, archris knight. This is Mathil of Grivear City and our friend Raskka the frushian. We bring urgent news. An army of thworfs and katzians are on their way, and they have already sacked Belthora. We are not sure if anyone is even alive in the city anymore."

The soldier licked his lips as he squinted down at the newcomers. "All right, open the gate!" he called down behind him.

As the gates swung open, Hondor was revealed in all of its majesty. Most houses were stone or wooden with thatched roofs, but they were closer together than Belthora, and the city spread itself out over three hills. Brown and tan were the prevailing colors of the city. Few gardens were found, but off to the east, Aron saw massive farmlands of wheat, corn, and livestock.

Raskka flew over the wall to meet with Aron and Mathil, resulting in many scowls from the soldiers. The sentry who greeted them before waited for the guests just within the gateway. "We heard rumors of a battle coming, but to hear Zontose's legions will be upon us shortly is grim news. Under whose authority did you report this?"

"King Ivo himself sent me."

"So he is dead, then?"

"I'm not sure. All I know is Belthora is on fire. How many escaped I cannot say, but we hope the same fate does not befall Hondor. We are here to help in any way."

"I am Commander Septin." The soldier extended his right hand to the knight. "We need all the help we can get, but I have to convey your message to the general before I can say exactly what role you guys will play in this mess."

"Then let's find him. We don't know how much time we have," Mathil commented.

"We …"

"Commander!" a sentry shouted, a slight waver in his voice. "A carriage is coming toward us. It looks like it might be the High King!"

"Is anyone else with him?" Aron asked.

"Not that I can tell. His carriage appears to be the only one."

Aron turned to the commander. "Then I will wait to speak with the king."

Ten minutes passed before the carriage rolled into Hondor. "Took you long enough, Hector!" Ivo shouted as he waddled down the steps of his vehicle.

"Apologies, sire."

"Your majesty." Aron bowed. "Are you the only one who escaped? What is the news from Belthora?"

Everyone nearby gazed expectantly at the king, but Ivo's face turned red, and he looked at the ground. "Hector, what takes you so long? Take care of the carriage, *now*."

"Yes, sire," Hector mumbled, whipping the reins. The four horses trotted off with the carriage trailing behind. Ivo unclasped his cloak and demanded a nearby soldier to fetch him some water. He then proceeded to walk further into the city. Aron hastened after him, and Mathil and Raskka followed. "Sire?" the knight pressed.

163

"What?" the king snapped.

"You didn't answer my questions. We need to know what happened. Is Belthora completely ruined?"

"Unfortunately for you, I am the king, and I do not have to answer to you, Aron."

"What aren't you telling me? Have you abandoned your people?" Aron's tone sharpened.

"You are no different, Aron. You will stop talking to me like this or I will have you arrested."

"I didn't abandon anyone," Aron retorted, ignoring Ivo's threat. "I am here to warn this city, but you left Belthora to save yourself, didn't you? Out of cowardice!"

"Belthora is lost!" Ivo shouted, his face now bright red and his eyes bulging from their sockets. "The thworfs quickly overran the city. If any are left alive, they will be enslaved. I tried to convince Locke to come with me, but he and his wife refused."

"So everyone is dead," Aron whispered.

"Yes, it is inevitable. Belthora was not prepared for such an attack. I didn't even fathom such a force would be sent by Zontose. Apparently what I saw was just a small portion of his army. Here at Hondor, though, we have a larger army, and maybe we will actually stand a chance."

"Maybe," Aron muttered as his gaze shifted to the lands beyond Hondor's wall.

The night dragged on, seemingly without end. Brome's mind reeled as he pondered the near success of his mission. *At last,* he thought with a smile across his thin lips. His heavy boots clomped down the hall, but his guest didn't notice. He stopped abruptly and placed a hand on her door, slowly twisting the knob. On the large bed within, Jori slept, holding a corner of her blanket tightly against her body. Dark eyes watched the little girl intently. "What is evil? Why do so many call me that?" Brome's hushed voice echoed.

"You remind me of someone I knew so long ago. I promised her that I would make the world safe again, and I did. I promised to rid Goandria of the festering virus that plagued us for so long, and that is exactly what I did. I saw that there was power and truth in our enemies, and I used that. I did what needed to be done. I am doing that again. I wish you could see that. I am power, and I deserve the respect of the people. Those who think they are following Voshnore are blind fools. Can they not see that He doesn't care? Can they not see that? I have transcended death and overcome all other obstacles. Do you people not see that sacrifice is a must whenever change occurs? Why does the desire to enact change and bring order to Goandria make me evil in the sight of so many?

"No matter," he sighed. "Very soon, the Three Republics will be no more. The wizards are rendered powerless and refuse to fight. A new era has already emerged, and you will help bring this about whether you want to or not. I want to free all people of Goandria from their ignorance. I want them to see that freedom is an illusion and that I am the lord and master they have needed. I want peace. I began this war to free the people from their entrapment, but they couldn't see it. I gave them a chance to submit and lay down their arms, but they wouldn't. Your special gift is key to this mess.

Someday you will need to trust me, Jori, in my true form. Someday you will see these people were wrong, and we will unite and bring order to our world. So many think I wish to destroy them, but that is not so. I wish to destroy their old beliefs and primitive ways." Jori began to stir in her sleep, so he turned and quietly closed the door.

Heavy steel-toed boots thudded along the nearly-abandoned hallways. A burgundy, hooded cloak with black edging flowed behind him as he marched on. His focus never strayed from the path before him, and his head remained high as he moved swiftly. A few thworf patrols snapped to attention as their lord walked by, but Zontose did nothing to acknowledge them. Down several flights of stairs he went. Once outside, his head finally turned to the right. A large window sprawled before him, revealing hundreds of thworfs still at work. Some bustled about the furnaces, working the bellows, striking iron, and fetching supplies. Others received the continuous shipments of food from the north.

He continued onward, returning to the depths of the fortress. As he entered the doorway of the circular chamber, the green flow of energy in the middle pulsated. The air in the room felt thick, a musty smell permeated the atmosphere, and as he drew near, the flow of energy pulsated with greater intensity. Zontose outstretched his trembling left hand. Just before he touched the flow of energy, his fingers curled, and he withdrew his hand. In that moment, the geyser's green energy flashed with streams of yellow and orange. Zontose stumbled back, cradling his head. The energy did not relent but steadily grew larger. The dark one crumbled against the back wall, snarling as he rocked back and forth, holding his head in both hands. The stone in the center turned red-orange, and the air became hot. "No! Agh, not again! Never again!" Zontose screamed. Clenching his fists, he bore his teeth and slowly rose to his feet. His eyes turned black, glowering at the geyser. "I have grown stronger. I will control it," he said under his breath, but the energy grew even more intense. Shockwaves erupted from the center, and each blast burned away more of Zontose's armor and clothing. A black cloud gathered around him. His skin became blacker than a moonless night. Stretching forth his arms, Zontose sent out an explosion of blackness, immediately calming the geyser.

The doors to the room burst open, and in marched Daest, followed by the rest of the osodars. "Master!" Daest exclaimed.

"I am fine." Zontose brushed him aside.

"The power …" began Daest.

Zontose raised his hand, immediately silencing the osodar. "Yes, I felt it too. I thought it was happening again, but …" his voice dropped as he reached into the now-still energy.

Darkness enveloped his mind's eye as his hand plunged into the geyser. There he saw himself alone in a blackness his eyes could not pierce. Thousands upon thousands of tiny lights steadily moved in formation across a landscape. As the darkness peeled away, he saw that the lights were torches held by his armies. The vision blurred and reformed into a sprawling city built of white stone, but many of the buildings now lay in rubble, and fires greedily devoured all in their wake. Belthora had been utterly defeated. Once again, the world blurred and then Hondor was visible. Thworfs mercilessly slaughtered their foes. The tide had turned forever against the Republics. "This is what I have already been told will come to pass. Why show me this?" Zontose asked, but he felt compelled to look deeper. His gaze could not shift away. A feeling crept up within him. His heart beat harder. Sweat began to bead upon his forehead. There was a blinding flash of white light, whiter than snow, and utterly piercing. Zontose attempted to shield his eyes, but the light still burned them through his eyelids and forearm. As quickly as the light came, it went out. The vision swirled into a myriad of colors before coalescing once again. Zontose saw his armies fleeing or destroyed. Everything went black again, and Zontose was flung backwards as the vision dissipated.

"It … can't … it can't be," Zontose mumbled as he stood back up.

"My lord, what did you see?" asked Daest.

Zontose's dark eyes bore into the osodar. "Utter and complete ruin. I do not understand. She said we would have total victory!"

"Defeat? How?"

"I am unsure. Victory was so certain."

"Perhaps it is just one possible future of many," Daest suggested.

"Hmm, yes, yes. The power is often mysterious," Zontose said quietly, more to himself than to his servant.

"What is your will, my lord?"

"We will go to Hondor and personally ensure our victory is complete."

"Master, that is what her ladyship warned us against! You were the one that convinced me of that. I implore you to rethink this."

168

Zontose swiftly faced the osodar again. His eyes narrowed, and his brow furrowed. "*You* implore *me*? Remember your place, Daest." He pointed a slender hand, and the osodar shrank back. "I will decided what we do. I am well aware of what I was told and once believed, but the vision I saw ... The vision I saw revealed nothing of our presence. Maybe it is time we show ourselves and our true power to the world. Maybe there is something Serinah missed. Maybe she only caught a glimpse of the future. I used to trust what she said without question, but ... with this new revelation I cannot allow my armies to be defeated at such a moment."

All the osodars knelt before Zontose and said in unison, "By your will and command, Lord Zontose."


The moon's light reflected off the city as masses of soldiers filed through the streets. Many helped to reinforce the walls, and others were placed in reserves behind the wall and in the city. A legion of cavaliers were tasked with evacuating the city, and within two hours, Hondor appeared to be nothing more than a military settlement. Crickets and other insects chirped and chattered as night's hold over Goandria became complete. Hundreds of torchlights dotted the city scape as men bustled about preparing the catapults, bracings for the gate, and reinforcements for the wall.

"What are we going to do now? The king has relinquished all control of the military, and he and the few remaining senators are walled up in the palace while the enemy is on our doorstep."

"I know, Mathil. Things are grim," Aron said quietly.

"Men are so much more cowardly than I could have imagined," Raskka added under her breath.

Mathil swiftly turned to face her. "Not all of us are. In fact, not all of any one group is the same. I'm sure you wouldn't like it if I said all frushians were bloodthirsty, ignorant savages?"

Raskka simply stared at the young man, frozen in place for some time. "You are right. You two are braver than anyone I have known before," she finally conceded, grasping Mathil in an embrace, then proceeding to do the same to Aron.

"In all seriousness, Aron, what is the next step? I mean, if we are all honest here, you are the most qualified to lead this army to victory."

"We need to see what the senate's plans are, if any. They are still in charge of the Republics." Aron sighed.

"Won't that be wasting time? The thworfs could be here any moment," Mathil protested.

"That is the proper way of things. No matter what you feel, I am not in charge, and I cannot make any final decisions."

"Good luck then. Somehow I feel you are going to need it."

Aron mounted his horse and rode to the palace. The building was stacked seven levels high with the eastern and western wings arcing back to the entry in a like a crescent moon. The structure itself had stone walls and a wooden roof that tapered to a point. Dozens of windows lined the face of the building with slender pillars separating each one. Unlike Belthora, nothing decorated the courtyard. There were only unkempt trees scattered from the palace to the roadway. *How Hondor is the seat of the Republics instead of Belthora is a mystery I will never understand,* thought Aron. The knight marched through the front door, the guards never flinching as he passed. The interior greeted him with a splash of gold and silver ornaments. A gold chandelier bearing three dozen red candles hung in the foyer. Beneath the light fixture, nine people talked amongst themselves, many making animated hand gestures as they spoke. One in particular repeatedly jabbed another in the shoulder with his index finger. All were dressed in dark blue robes, save for one. The corpulent Ivo could not be mistaken, even after changing into green, gold, and black robes.

"Senators," Aron muttered, rolling his eyes.

"The king has lost all rights to rule. He has been an incompetent fool all along. If he was no longer in charge, the war would have been over," a gray-haired woman complained.

"He was elected by the people! We cannot change that!" another gray-haired woman exclaimed.

"The thworfs are on our doorstep. We need to figure out what to do and how to do it before our fates are decided for us," a male senator interjected.

On the other side of the room, another cluster of senators bickered amongst each other. "The senate should have taken the authority to rule once the war began. The elected kings have foolishly sat idle while Zontose carved out large swaths of territory. Now it is only a matter of time before the thworfs raze Hondor as well."

"Oh, do be quiet, Olin. Your lust for power has always been obvious. The Republics were built in such a way that no portion of government can have too much power."

"But the king *has* the power. The senate has had little authority in the matters of warfare for two years now! Ivo has not heeded our warning, and here we find he consulted with the enemy and nearly handed over our soldiers!"

While all this transpired around Ivo, he did not seem to pay any heed. He poured himself a tankard of ale and sat at a large table, watching the political show before him.

"Excuse me!" he called out. No one seemed to hear. "Excuse me!" the knight shouted a second time. All conversations were silenced.

"Who dares?" another middle-aged man demanded.

"Someone who does not wish to see another city fall," Aron responded. All eyes were upon him, many contorted into frowns. "I am Aron, archris knight of the village Fair Wood in Grivear. We need to take action now! We need to organize the troops and have a firm plan in place."

One senator snapped, "We do not take orders or suggestions from you. Do you not see that we have already evacuated the city? Our troops are diligently working hard to prepare the city. Take your unsolicited advice elsewhere."

"That is not enough! We need to protect this city. Where will all those people go if every city is destroyed? Surely Zontose will round them up and enslave them, or worse. You cannot haphazardly expect your military leaders to prepare the city when they need real direction. Protecting Hondor is crucial to the survival of the Republics and its people." Aron balled his hand into a fist as his spoke.

A silver-haired man with a mid-length beard marched in through the palace doors. He stood in the doorway, back fully straight, eyes surveying the room, and helm propped under his left arm. The senators all turned to him. "General Wilkin, to what do we owe this honor?" a senator asked.

"The thworf army has been spotted. The knight was correct. Belthora seems to be in utter ruin. What is your command?" the general's deep voice reverberated.

The senators all looked at one another, but no answer came. General Wilkin's eyes narrowed. "What have you fools been doing this whole time?" Again no answer came.

"Your majesty." Wilkin turned to Ivo. "What is going on here?"

"The senate removed me from power. Our world is broken and at an end. Go and do whatever you will."

"This is what the glorious Republics have become?" Wilkin's voice grew louder, eyeing each person in the room.

"How many soldiers do you have?" Aron came forward.

"Nearly three-thousand infantry and less than two-thousand cavalry."

"That won't be enough."

"You are Aron?" the general asked, glancing at the knight's weapon.

"I am."

"In that case, it is an honor to meet you. Archris knights are in short supply these days." Wilkin clasped Aron's right hand.

"The honor is mine, sir."

"It is short notice, but would you command the men along the wall? Few here have the expertise of an archris knight, and the wall is our first defense. I will need someone of your caliber up there."

"I will go where ever I am needed. I also came here with a young man from Grivear City and a frushian. They will also help in this fight in any way they can."

"A frushian?" asked Wilkin.

"They are a people from Hallow Forest."

"I need soldiers. How will this frushian she fare in a fight?"

"I believe she would do well," Aron said with a slight smile.

"And the boy?"

"He is far more inexperienced, but he has a strong heart."

"I'm sure an opportunity will present itself for him as well. We will all have to fight in some capacity," the general said solemnly.

"General, I am at your service, but if I may, I think a new approach is needed to defend Hondor," said Aron with a slight twinkle in his eye.

"Is that so? I would love to hear your ideas."


The blackness of night was still upon Goandria, but dawn was near. Zontose's armies marched over the plains. Thousands upon thousands of leather and steel clad feet stomped along. Black dragons roared and drums pounded as the army closed in. At the base of Hondor's wall, all available riders waited. General Wilkin rode to the front of the lines and surveyed his troops. He raised his long bow before the men. "Tonight our enemy makes his move against us, and he intends to wipe out all who oppose him. Belthora has fallen, Grivear City is fallen, villages are being burned, and on top of all this, our leaders squabble and bicker, and our High King cowers in fear. The times are grim, soldiers of Ashear, but do not lose hope! We are a strong people! The Republics have not yet been defeated, nor will they while men like you still fight for them. We fight not just for the Republics but for our wives, our children, our friends, our parents, and for everyone we have ever loved and do not wish to see enslaved to Zontose. We represent them all on the battlefield today!"

"For the Republics!" Aron cried out. The rest of the soldiers responded, "For the Republics!"

Zontose's armies halted their advance. Blue eyes looked over the soldiers and their great steeds. Gray lips curled, revealing sharp fangs and missing teeth. Soot-covered fingers stroked a black beard that ran along the neck. *What is this? The fools now decide to come out from behind their walls and meet us?* the creature thought. Its face contorted into what one may call a smile.

"General Cshar, shall I send in my men?" the commander of the northmen asked.

"No, not yet. Bring up the prisoners."

Four thworfs cracked their whips across the backs of fifty men whose hands and feet were chained. A few of the men had severed hands or arms, and all were bloodied

175

and bruised. Their armor and shirts had been removed, and their backs dripped with blood. As they were forced to move, some begged for mercy, but their pleas were met with a sword.

"Release them," Cshar ordered. The prisoners' chains were unlocked, and the hapless men were shoved forward.

"What are they doing?" Aron wondered, straining his eyes.

"Archers, stand ready!" Wilkin ordered. Immediately, hundreds of arrows were notched.

"Wait, something doesn't feel right," Aron called out to the general.

"What do you mean?" Just as the words left Wilkin's mouth, the enemy's arrows began pelting the men racing toward them.

"I think those are our men! Quick, flank the enemy and draw their fire," Aron commanded before the general could get a word in. Five hundred horsemen split off from the main group. Half rode toward the western portion of Zontose's army while the others rode to the east. Within minutes, the Hondor cavalry closed in around the former captives, hurling arrows down upon the thworfs.

"Sir, why did you let them go?" asked a thworf captain, grimacing at the sight before him.

"Because I can." Cshar smirked.

"Gather the prisoners and pull back!" Wilkin called out, hoping the men would hear him over the din of battle. The nearby cavaliers each grabbed a former prisoner, hauled them onto the backs of their steeds, and trampled off back to Hondor. Some of the remaining horsemen leveled their spears into the mass of thworfs, and others continued to fire arrows upon them.

As Aron's troops rode to safety, General Wilkin drew his broadsword. "Ride now! For Hondor, for freedom! We ride through the heart of the army and then return. Just focus on getting through and taking out as many as you can. Remember what is at stake, friends. Remember what we are fighting for, and think about what kind of future we want to leave behind for our children!" He rode to the west, and the remaining horsemen followed. Six thousand hooves trampled to the far western edge of Zontose's armies and arced north, heading for the very core of the enemy forces.

Just as the soldiers of Hondor moved in, ten katzians marched forward and then halted. They lined up to wait for the horsemen, their duel blades pointing outward. Hondor arrows rained down upon the katzians, but they merely glanced off their armor. A few projectiles managed to hit between the joints of the armor, but the katzians who were affected did not flinch. They appeared to be bronze and steel emblazoned statues as the arrows continued to rain down.

The knights pressed on until they were right before the katzians. They threw spears or slashed with their swords, but the giants did not move. Bewildered, the knights of Hondor pressed on through the thworf ranks.

When about half of the horsemen had passed the katzians, their swords suddenly came alive, whirling like windmills as they slaughtered dozens of Hondor in each stroke. Much of the cavalry turned to face the katzians. Looking back, Aron's heart sank, and his mouth hung open as he watched the carnage. "What is Wilkin doing?

He is going to get all those men killed!" The thworfs suddenly organized themselves. Tightening their formation and withdrawing their weapons, they wildly slashed at the attackers. General Wilkin was completely surrounded, and more katzians and thworfs moved in on his location.

"Retreat!" Wilkin ordered, finally able to break free as several soldiers came to his aid. A few hundred horsemen had made it through to the other side of the thworf army, and those contending with the katzians broke away. Zontose's forces marched forward, following Hondor's retreating soldiers. Just as the city gates closed behind the last of the cavaliers, the archers along the wall unleashed their arrows. Siege ladders were hurriedly hoisted up, and swarms of thworfs climbed up. Aron hurried to the top of the wall, his sword at the ready. Few thworfs made it very far up their ladders before they fell to the blades of archris knights.

"Aron!" a male voice called out. "Aron!" The knight turned and saw the commander. "Sir, one of the men you freed is asking for you."

"Commander, I'm not sure this is the time. If we live through the night ..."

"Sir, he was rather insistent."

"Fine, take me to him." Aron re-sheathed his blade.

The officer hastily moved to the medical facility of Hondor. The building was a small wood shelter with a thatched roof. Five columns carved with elongated leaf designs ran along each side. Aron walked up the creaky stairs and opened the red-stained door. Inside, the returned prisoners were all laying on cots. "He is this way." The commander led Aron to the back of the building. As the man laying down turned, Aron knew immediately who it was. "Quartose!" he cried out, instantly embracing his friend.

As the fight for Hondor began, Mathil walked slowly down a narrow stone street. His head was down, and he occasionally kicked a rock along the road. He did not know how long he had been walking. His chest felt like a half-dozen large stones lay upon it, his eyes were red, and his shoulder muscles remained tense as he walked on. All around him, soldiers were running amok, some were on horses shouting orders, and others ran to lend aid where needed, sometimes bumping into the young man. *What am I doing here? I can't help them. Look, they are soldiers, trained from birth. What can I do? Maybe Aron was right. Maybe I am not ready to fight in this war. I have hardly any training. They gave me a sword but how can I use it?* Mathil thought as his feet shuffled along.

Flashes of light caught the corner of his eye. Turning to see what it was, Mathil saw that a portion of the wall was now on fire. Men rushed over with buckets of water, trying to contain the blaze, but their efforts seemed vain. The wooden city easily succumbed to the fire, which quickly spread. Still, the warriors pressed on, and no thworf managed to get past the wall. "It's only a matter of time before they start swarming Hondor like bees." Mathil quietly turned forward. Before him rose a mighty stone building with a tapered roof and a spire on each corner. In the very center of the roof rose a bell tower, making the structure stand taller than any in the area. Even amidst the battle, two-guards stood silently on either side of the entrance.

His curiosity peaked, Mathil decided to venture into the building. To his surprise, the guards did not seem bothered by his presence, and they did not move to stop him. He wrapped his fingers around the handle and slowly opened the door. Mathil saw no one inside. The floor was covered in rugs depicting people relating to the heavens. One showed a woman on her knees with sala dancing around her as the sky radiated with beams of yellow, orange, and violet. Each unique rug was about ten yards by four yards, and eleven of them ran along the floor leading to an altar. Seven purple candles were lit along a stone railing that lined the holy area. The altar itself was held up by granite columns four inches wide and two-feet tall. Two statues stood in the back, each twice the height of a man. They were armored, and their swords pointed inward, highlighting a tapestry. Mathil moved closer, his fingers brushing the silky fabric of the tapestry. It depicted a fiery being whose yellow, orange, and red body glistened as if Mathil could see the fire actually moving. The background was violet. Nothing else accented the being, but the sparkling threads composing the creature completely captivated Mathil's attention.

He collapsed to his knees, his tear-filled eyes still locked on the tapestry. "Where are You? Can You not see that Your people are suffering? Don't You care? How can You allow that monster to have so much power?

"Answer me!" he yelled. "What does it take for You to show yourself? We are all about to die. We are backed into a corner with nowhere else to run. Zontose's army is so … so large … so very large …"

As he wept bitterly, his eyes bore holes into the fabric before him. "I was taught that You are love, that You will ultimately protect your people. I don't see it anymore. There is so much evil, and You have done nothing!"

"Who are you talking to?" a high-pitched voice suddenly asked.

Mathil swiftly turned around and saw a small boy, maybe five or six years old, standing at the other end of the temple.

"I … uh …" Mathil stammered.

"You are so loud! Mommy always says I need to play quietly when I play pretend," the little boy said matter-of-factly.

"I wasn't playing pretend."

"Then who were you talking to?"

Mathil eyes shifted to the tapestry once again. "Voshnore," he said softly.

"Oh?" The boy's eyes lit up. "I talk to him a lot. He told me that everything is going to be okay tonight."

"Did He? Did He tell you why He allowed so many good soldiers to die?"

"No, just that things will be all right."

"Hmm," Mathil snorted.

"Well, He does see more than we do," the boy said indignantly.

"I suppose."

"Who are you?" asked the child. "You don't look like a soldier."

"My name is Mathil, and no, I'm not a soldier."

"My daddy is a soldier. I was hiding when everyone left. I didn't want to leave him."

A smile stretched across Mathil's lips. His eyes softened as he looked at the boy standing before him. The boy was so small in spite of his courage. "I thought I could fight, but I don't think I can," Mathil said.

"Why are you afraid?" The boy tilted his head.

"I never said I was afraid. I said I can't." His eyes narrowed for a brief moment. "Besides, I do not have to answer to a child."

"So then, why can't you?" the boy pressed, undeterred.

"I am not skilled enough. I will just get in everyone's way."

"Huh, but you are a grown up."

"Maybe," Mathil said softly.

"I think you are just afraid. I get scared too, but I didn't know big people did too."

"Maybe." Mathil shrugged. "Maybe I am afraid, afraid to fail my parents, my friends, Voshnore …"

"Aren't you mad at Him?"

"Huh?" Mathil's face contorted for a brief second.

"Well, you were just yelling at Him."

Fire shot though his chest. "Yes, I suppose I was."

"Maybe you just need to trust that everything is going to work out. Even grown-ups can only know so much."

"You know, maybe you are right. After all, I wanted to be here. You said your dad is a soldier? Does he know you are still in Hondor?"

The boy's face turned red, and he looked down at his feet. "Uh, not exactly."

Mathil withdrew his long dagger. "Do you know where to find a place to hide in here?"

The boy nodded.

"Do you know how to use this?"

Again the boy nodded. "Uh huh, I started my knight training with Daddy a year ago," he said proudly.

"I still have my sword. Take this and find a place to hide. If the thworfs find you, use the dagger. If you see fire, run as fast as you can away from the city."

"Okay, Mr. Mathil." The boy hastily grabbed the weapon and raced up a flight of stairs to the far left of the altar.

"Please, Voshnore, keep him safe. If You truly do have a plan, please, let no harm come to that child," he whispered, unsheathing his weapon before stepping back outside. Smoke and ash were everywhere. The clash of steel on steel rang in the distance. Mathil didn't see any thworfs yet, which he took as a good sign. Gripping his weapon tightly, he took a deep breath and swiftly stepped forward, propelled himself toward the fighting.

Like thousands of spiders, the thworfs continued to swarm up the ladders and through broken sections of the wall. Hondor's army continued to push back. Archer reserves launched volleys upon volleys of arrows, decimating the thworf ranks, but they still scrambled forward over their fallen. The infantry's weapons met their foes like scythes to grass, but as more katzians moved in with their trebuchets, the Hondor military began pulling back.

Raskka stood at the top of the wall, her daggers ceaselessly spinning as they tore through thworf flesh. A smile cracked her hard face as she fought. Thworf after thworf came rushing at her, seemingly unaware of the sheer volume of their kind that lay at the frushian's feet. Her wide, fiery eyes dazzled in the moonlight, challenging all opponents to just try to overtake her. "Is this the best you can do?" she giggled madly, killing two more thworfs simultaneously. Then, without warning, the flow of thworfs near her stopped. Some even turned to run, but as they turned, orbs of fire erupted against their backs, instantly incinerating them.

"That's right, run you cowards!" she screamed. The wall began to shake. *Thud, thud, thud,* loose supports began to crumble on the already damaged structure. Massive helms peeked up from the ladders lining the wall, rising double the size of any thworf's. "Katzians!" she breathed. "Now I've got a challenge," she roared. The Hondor soldiers in the vicinity slowly backed away. When the nearest katzian had just placed her feet upon the top of the wall, Raskka hurled a stream of fire from her hands, roasting the huge creature within its armor.

The other soldiers cheered as the katzian fell. Many prepared their bows, and Raskka ignited their arrows. "Push them back!" Raskka shouted. Fire arrows and magic peppered the katzians, hindering their advance. *Whoosh,* all the fires in the city went suddenly out. *Flap, flap,* the sound of dozens of wings caught Raskka's ear. The men around her did not appear to notice, as everyone seemed to be reeling from the shock of what had happened. However, Raskka's orange-yellow eyes could not shift away from the creatures in the distance, for upon their backs she could have sworn she saw glowing blue eyes. Her heart quickened its beating. A bone-penetrating chill ran down her back as she watched them. Her mind began to fog, and a crushing, cold feeling enveloped her. Raskka crumbled to her knees, her eyes still locked on the dragon riders. "What are you?" she whispered. Rivulets slowly trickled from the corners of her eyes, not knowing what new horrors awaited Hondor.

# Chapter 11

Below, Belthora smoldered, flames still licked the stone, and massive plumes of ash filled the air, raining black snow upon the ground. Gloved hands grasped the reins of the flying steed. Its breath sounded raspy, and once in a while, the creature snorted and growled. Seventeen others flanked the beast on either side, but this one was longer, and its wings were twice as wide. Its green eyes slowly moved side to side, surveying the ground as it flew. The vertical slit for a pupil dilated as its focus shifted to another region. The great beast's eyelids narrowed, and its wings flapped harder. "You see it, too. Don't worry. We will get there in time," the rider consoled. The creature simply grunted and continued its pace.

Hondor soon became visible. Like Belthora, fire and ash belched from the city, but only in the regions closest to the wall. Zontose locked eyes with the osodar nearest to him, slowly nodded to his servant, and drew the dragon's reins. As Zontose fell back behind the rest, Daest raised his hands to the sky, and a blue vortex began to swirl between his out stretched fingertips. The rest of the osodars lifted their hands as well, and the vortex gradually grew larger. Bits of snow formed in the eye of the vortex, and frost began to accumulate along the dragons' scales. Zontose reached forward and launched a network of yellow energy beams to the dragons, binding them all in a web.

"Release!" Zontose commanded, and the vortex exploded outward toward Hondor. The web of energy dispersed.

"Fools. They fight like they can win," Daest commented.

"Maybe they believe they can win, but no one can save them," Zontose replied, once again riding in the front. "They chose this for themselves. They chose to rebel against progress, against a better life in which a better lord rules them. They believe they have freedom, but free will is merely an illusion."

A light suddenly appeared in the sky above Hondor. Zontose squinted, at first thinking it nothing more than a star, but it continued to grow in size and in brightness. The light was the color of snow, but more pure than anything Zontose had seen. It became even whiter as the spot grew into a disk shape over the city.

"What is that, master?" Daest gasped.

Zontose said nothing, his mouth open as he watched. From the disk, rivers of white pulsated through the sky. A curtain of light blasted down from these rivers and erupted with a massive pulse of purity. The pulse hurdled the dragons into a hillside. Then the rivers of light disappeared, and a light blue hue rimmed the disk above Hondor. Zontose slowly regained his footing. His dragon lay sprawled out on its back, and some of the other smaller dragons had broken their necks or wings. Stumbling forward and grasping the side of his steed for support, Zontose looked off toward the strange anomaly in the sky. He moved to brush himself off, but he realized that all of his armor had been burned away. The osodars were now thin, translucent figures. They resembled skeletons with a glowing yellow aura around them, for their robes had been burned away as well. Their eyes burned even brighter as they looked off to the city, unconcerned with anything else. "What is this new power? Why does it challenge me?" Zontose whispered under his breath. The answer came: Two dozen beings floated down from the white disk.

"I can't believe you are alive!" Aron gasped, hugging his friend once again.

"Ah, careful," Quartose moaned.

"What happened?"

Quartose shook his head. "It was ... horrible. Thworfs, death, fire. It was everywhere. Everything is a jumbled mess. I remember seeing King Locke fighting to the death with his guards as the thworfs swarmed into the city ... " A cold blast swept through the medical facility, immediately extinguishing all candlelight and shaking the walls of the building. "What was that?" Quartose perked up.

Aron glanced outside. "I don't know."

"You should go check it out. We will catch up later." The other knight smiled weakly.

"I don't want to leave you again. Quartose, I never told you before, but I'm sorry. I'm sorry for taking Nina and Jori's deaths out on you. I'm sorry I was so hard on you."

Quartose clasped his friend's hand. "Aron, you have been through a lot. You have suffered in ways I could not imagine. The war has taken more from you than from anyone else I know, and I want you to know that I forgave you a long time ago. Now go. Hondor needs you more than I do right now."

Aron forced a smile again, then turned and hurried out of the medical facility. Death was everywhere. The waning night seemed to offer no relief from its bitter darkness. "Where is the sun?" he pondered as he looked upon the eastern sky. He felt a hand upon his left shoulder. "I hear we have a battle to win," a young voice said.

"Mathil, if you just now heard that, I'm afraid you are far more dense than I thought possible." The knight grinned.

"So what's the plan?"

"You decided you are fighting now?"

"Eh, better late than never, but you were right. Making the decision to fight in a war is far different when the fighting actually starts."

"What stopped you?"

"Fear that I'm not good enough. I'm still afraid. I want to help, not be in the way."

"We all feel that way." Aron's head cocked a bit. "Wait, what is that?" He pointed to the sky.

"It looks like just a star. A really big one ... Wait, is it growing?"

"Yes, it is." Aron backed up.

"What do you think it might be?" Mathil asked.

"It is nothing I have ever seen before. Perhaps it is some device of Zontose? Whatever it is, it's right above us."

"Ugh, it's so bright!" Mathil moaned, shielding his eyes.

"Come, let's find shelter," Aron suggested.

The white light absorbed everything, rendering it nearly impossible to see. "Ah, my eyes!" Mathil shrieked, burying his closed eyes in his hands in an attempt to find relief. "What the heck is going on here?" he shouted, crumbling to the ground. The light suddenly diminished in intensity, and Mathil slowly removed his hands from his eyes. The piercing light was still smothering Hondor, and now a massive white disk hung in the sky above the city.

"Aron, things just got crazier." The young man pointed skyward.

The knight's eyes shifted up, growing wide. His chest felt heavy, and he found himself on his knees, not remembering how he got there. Tears streamed down his dirty cheeks as he watched the sky break open in a dazzling light show. Mathil shook Aron gently. "Aron! Aron!" But there was no response. A few seconds passed, then Aron crumbled to the ground, weeping hysterically.

"Aron!" Mathil shouted again. His brows raised a bit, and his voice shrill. The young man's heart pounded wildly, not knowing what had overcome the knight. "Help!" he shouted out, but all around him people had collapsed in tears as well. Finally, Mathil felt strange blend of peace, holiness, and fear weigh down upon him. Mathil fell to his knees like the others. His hands trembled, and he suddenly felt very small and powerless, but also immensely loved and cherished. Where this feeling came from, he could not say. It seemed external, but at the same time it filled every part of his being. The emotion was so foreign, but it felt as if his father's arms wrapped around him with a great intensity.

190

His mind went back to just moments before when he was in the temple. He saw himself yelling and blaming Voshnore for the evils he saw, and he was filled with shame. Taking a moment to gaze up through his tear-filled eyes, he saw something that he could not explain and his eyes could not believe. Twenty-four beings descended from the disk of light. They were large, about twice the size of an average person, and covered from head to toe in silver armor and purple robes. As they came down, Mathil struggled to make out what they were through the glow of the disk. They appeared to be made of pure light with a violet hue. "Can it be?" he uttered. "Have they come to save us?"

As the beings came from the heavens, Raskka and the men who fought beside her stood utterly motionless. A terrible pressure lay upon her, the same as the others, yet she continued to stand. The fighting completely stopped. The thworfs gazed up at the newcomers in awe, but the katzians held their ground. Their hard eyes glowered at the beings as they raced down to the battlefield. Then a bow twanged, followed by hundreds of others. Thworf arrows whistled toward the creatures. "No!" Raskka yelped, falling to her knees, but all the arrows glanced off their targets.

Like lightning, the beings rocketed to the ground, causing a massive shockwave. Dozens of thworfs were thrown backward. Standing in a ring, they withdrew their two-handed swords simultaneously. The weapons were twice as tall as the creatures, broad, glistening white, and rimmed with a pale-yellow flame. The disk in the sky evaporated, and the radiant glow from the beings dimmed, revealing their crystalline bodies that radiated like liquid silver. Pairs of bright green, blue, and orange eyes unblinkingly pierced all who looked upon them. "Praise Voshnore! The sala have come to save us!" someone announced. Throughout the city all rose to their feet, clambering to get a closer look at the divine warriors.

One particular sala stood taller than the rest. Bronze locks flowed over his shoulders and down his back. "Slaves of Zontose, leave at once. Never trouble the Republics again, and never serve the will of your master again, for only ruin awaits those who align themselves with Zontose," his bass voice resounded, sending tremors through ground. The thworfs backed away, still holding their weapons. Some hastily looked to their comrades, but no one said anything to the sala. "This is your warning. Flee now." Minutes passed as the thworfs and sala glared at one another, waiting for one side to make the first move.

Finally, a large and muscular thworf came forward. "We serve Zontose, the lord and god of all! All who challenge him will be crushed." The thworfs quickly advanced on the sala. Arrows whirred through the air once again. Many of the thworfs were bisected by one stroke of a sala's weapon, others that simply stood too near burst into flames, and some were sent flying backwards, but none could come near enough to even scratch the sala with a sword. Within minutes, hundreds of thworfs were slaughtered. Some dropped their weapons and fled, but others continued their assault, only to be struck down like the others.

Then the katzians moved in slowly and steadily, ready to test their metal against a new foe. A score of the feline creatures closed in around the circle of sala, their dual claymores at the ready. The sala wasted no time. They fanned outward in unison, smiting the mighty katzians with a single blow. They continued to fan outward amidst the army, violet fire trailing behind them.

The men of Dalarashess scattered, riding quickly away from the seemingly invincible foe. Many of the steeds bucked off their riders and trampled off through the grasslands, mad with fear. Without their horses, some of the men were forced to throw down their arms and surrender. Some of the thworfs refused to give up against the sala, but most ran away screeching madly. The katzians continued their wild assault, but eventually all were defeated.

The black dragons swarmed down, gushing jets of fire upon the sala. Three sala leapt to the sky, growing larger. A brilliant, fiery light emanated from their being. Silvery blades blurred through the air, felling several dragons within moments.

During the fight, the horizon became streaked with red and orange rays as the long darkness finally gave way to the morning light. The thworfs within Hondor were not ready to give up yet, for the spell of confusion had broken, and they knew their time was limited. While their comrades fled from the sala, the enemy within the walls pushed back even harder against the defenders. Black swords hammered against the men of Hondor. The wide-eyed and gaunt-faced thworfs cast aside their shields and helmets. Hondor soldiers quickly composed themselves, no longer able to be dazzled by the sala's arrival. The din of steel on steel and cries of death filled the city once more.

One thworf picked up the weapon of a fallen kinsmen. With a sword in each hand, he approached a sala. "You have won today, sky-god, but as great as your power is, Zontose is the true god! Zontose will kill you all," he screamed.

The sala merely cocked its head. Its eyes flared as the thworf spoke. "This is the fate of your master and all who serve him. You have been duped, thworf." Then it struck the creature down.

Tears once again welled in Aron's eyes as he witnessed the final victory unfold. "Thank you." He looked to the sky, but the words felt so weak. He was prepared to die, and in the deepest pit of his heart, he had believed the Republics would fall and that Voshnore had abandoned them.

Beside Aron stood Mathil and Raskka. Their jaws hung open, and their eyes were wide as they gazed at the impossible situation before them. "Who are these sala?" Raskka asked, staring hypnotically. "They are so beautiful ..."

"Soldiers of Voshnore," Aron said simply.

"Never have I seen such majesty, such power, such *potency*," she said. "I feel a connection to them, as I have not felt before. Almost like we are kin."

Mathil turned to her. "How could that be?" Aron, however, seemed to ignore the comment as the final remnant of Zontose's army fled.

"I'm not sure. My people are all tuned in to the world of the spirits, but this feels so much different. Maybe the sala are kindred spirits of the goddess, or maybe she created them, or something. I just don't know."

"I seriously doubt they have any connection to your goddess," Mathil said bluntly, immediately regretting the words.

Raskka glared at the young man. "You may not believe as I do, but the goddess is the one that brought me to find you."

"I'm sorry, I didn't mean …"

"Of course you did, otherwise you wouldn't have said it."

"I speak first and think later most of the time. I really am sorry."

"I shouldn't have snapped at you either. We all say foolish things from time to time. Perhaps you do more than others, but I shouldn't have reacted so harshly." Raskka smirked.

"You are probably right." Mathil returned the smile.

"Everything looks like it is taken care of here. I think it is time I seek the goddess's will and find my own path. Maybe someday I will return to my people."

"You're leaving? I thought you had nowhere else to go."

"When I said that, I didn't because my role was to help you and to learn."

"Then let me come with you. I don't have anywhere to go. Everyone I loved was killed, and I don't want to be alone anymore."

Raskka's eyes shifted to Aron, her face lighting up as she spoke. "You aren't alone." Then she ignited her wings and shot to the sky, leaving Mathil to watch as she flew north.

The sun now shone brightly in the fresh morning sky, and birds sang melodies of welcome to the new day. Zontose's soldiers had either retreated or been defeated. The victory over Zontose was absolute, and it seemed even the heavens rejoiced. The clear blue sky was dotted with an occasional puffy cloud, and a cool breeze invigorated every breath. None could believe what had transpired, for most had expected the previous night to be their last. There was weeping in the streets and songs of praise to Voshnore, but the victory had been bitter-sweet. Even though Hondor and the Republics still lived, many Hondor and archris knights perished, more than any could count. Aron slowly walked down the steps from the wall top to the city. At his feet, humans and thworfs lay scattered all around.

The knight noticed a sala approaching him. Aron instantly fell to his knees. "Thank you," he gasped. His chest tightened, and his heart leapt from the presence and the feeling of such intense love. He felt like he could pass out at any moment.

"Rise, knight of Grivear. Do not bow to me or any of us, for we are just servants."

Aron slowly rose, but he was unable to look at the sala's face. "Why now? Why come at all? Why even let Zontose gain the power he did?" Aron's mouth spewed without warning, taking even himself by surprise.

The sala simply rested his hand on Aron's shoulder. The knight looked up and saw a gentle smile spread across the sala's face. "There are many things you will not understand. We come at a pivotal moment, but it is up to the people to defend Goandria, just as it always has been. This will be the last time we intervene directly

196

in this war. Aron," its tone suddenly sharpened, "there is a greater darkness behind all this, and you and everyone in Goandria will be tested."

"Tested how?" But Aron's question was answered only with a searing light that radiated forth from the sala. Seconds later, they all vanished.

# Epilogue

All eyes were on him as he heaved his massive body onto the makeshift stage comprised of several upturned barrels and two twelve-foot by four-foot planks of wood. The wood groaned under the pressure, but resolved to hold under the strain. Brown eyes set in a gray-bearded face looked the crowd over, the expression strangely listless with a hint of glee. "People of Hondor!" His voice echoed. "We are in dark times, but I'm sure that is not news to you, for it has been a week since the loss of Belthora and many warriors in our own city. It has been a week since the sala unexpectedly delivered us, saving our city and civilization from utter ruin. There has been deep darkness and bright light at every turn. We each have lost so much. People we treasured are now gone, some of our homes are now ashes and splinters, and on top of all this, the armies that protected us have been diminished significantly. Yet the sala saved us! We praise Voshnore for His providence, but the sala have warned some of you that we are on our own now as we have always been. We cannot count on another miraculous save.

"So the question is, now what? You, the people, have returned to your city only to find it a pale shadow of its former glory. The senators who deemed me a coward are missing! The wizards have somehow managed to ignore this entire war, completely abandoning their task of protecting Goandria. What does it take to get their attention? Or are they content with reading and writing scrolls while the world burns around them? And as far as

I can see, every village and city in the Republics has been destroyed by Zontose. What exactly are we left with? What took the sala so long? Why save us at the very last second? There are so many unknowns, and I do not have the answers to these questions. I was elected to be your High King, but there are no Republics to govern. All that remains of the Three Republics is this city, and I promise to protect you and to build up our defenses so that if Zontose comes at us again, we will be ready! We will look for survivors beyond these walls and fortify our military, our civilization. Zontose can have the husk of the Republics. Within this city, we will restore the memory and glory of the Republics!"

Cries burst throughout Hondor, "Ivo! Ivo! Long live Hondor!"

Elsewhere, Jori lay sleeping in her bed, but it was during this time that she saw the most. At first, she saw bright, swirling fog which looked like it produced its own energy, for Jori did not see sun, moon, or torches anywhere. The bright clouds were all around, as far as she could see. The warmth of the light rejuvenated her soul, and she began to weep, but she was uncertain why. The girl crumbled to her knees, and her heart leapt with a love so profound, she did not know such love was even possible.

She heard a gentle voice. *Be patient my child. All things happen in their own time. Stay strong. You are not as alone as you think you are. I see everything. You do not need to worry. Sometimes people must endure a little bad in their lifetime. If only you could see more than you do, you would not worry or be afraid.* Then the light was gone. Anger flared within Jori, already forgetting the peace she had just experienced. "Patient? Why am I here? Why won't anyone save me?" she yelled and stomped her foot, but she was left with silence, alone and confused.

Goandria unfolded before her eyes. She saw forests, grasslands, and deserts. Jori could not believe the size of the world before her, realizing that she only knew a small corner of it. Then, she saw herself sleeping. On one side of her, there was a great white light. On the other was a darkness so deep that it looked like no light could penetrate it. Her vision swirled into a marbled mess of light and dark then coalesced to show two armies fighting for the very fate of Goandria. Thousands had fallen on both sides, and blood completely soaked the ground. Neither side appeared to notice the carnage and death, for they fought without relent. Time slowed, and suddenly the warriors were frozen. Jori saw two old towers, and somehow she knew the people within them were wizards, crying out for help. The little girl could feel their agony. Tears once more rolled down her red cheeks.

Again the vision changed. Jori saw a man sitting alone in a small wooden house. A fire crackled beside him as he hurriedly scribbled something on a piece of parchment. He had long, light-colored, unkempt hair and a wild expression, but his eyes revealed a hidden wisdom. Jori studied the man with renewed wonder. She saw him rising above the Blessed Temples, and the wizards came out, cheering and praising Voshnore. Jori noticed something different about the man she first saw alone by the fire. He had a glow about him, something like yellow fire rimming his whole body, but it did not burn. *This one has been chosen. He has a bigger destiny than he can ever comprehend*, Jori heard an ominous but kindly voice say, but she was unsure who spoke.

"Who are you?" Jori called out.

*Someone who knows you and loves you. Soon you will find me, but you must do it on your own. You must want to be with me.*

Jori's eyes opened, her heart pumped quickly, and her small hands trembled as she rubbed her eyes. The memory of what she had just dreamt was already fading, and just a few minutes later, she could only recall vague images and feelings. Jori did not know it, but the vision she had seen was unique, for she was not the only one to have seen it.

Miles away to the southeast, a wizard lay asleep. He saw the same horrible scenes. Then, he saw something that Jori did not. Wizards prayed without ceasing for their plight to be over. Doubt spread across Goandria in the form of a violet flame that consumed everything in its wake: doubt that the wizards would uphold their oath to Goandria, doubt that freedom was possible, doubt that there was hope at all. Rising out of the purple fire was the specter wolf that had attacked them at the beginning of the war. Snarling, it reared its fiery head and belched a black ooze onto a battlefield, laughing like a human.

The wizard called out, "Harkendor!" He felt rage build up inside of him, knowing he was looking at the great traitor. The one that once led the wizards to victory against the worlox was now the very embodiment of evil. Harkendor, the foresworn wizard who tried to undo everything their order had stood for, and even nearly defeated them, now was before him. The wizard clenched his jaw and stared down his enemy. Whether it was bravery or madness that drove him, he did not know. "Harkendor!" he yelled again. "You will answer for your crimes! You will not be able to contain us forever."

Harkendor was silent, but the laughter continued for several more seconds, fading away into the blackness. The specter turned into the form of a dark warrior. The wizard shifted, trying to get a better look, but Harkendor's new form blurred. Suddenly, the rough, charcoal skin faded and smoothed, and he began to look more like a man than a monstrous creature. Confused and intrigued, the wizard continued to watch, dumbfounded to see Lorkai's form before him. Then the vision turned to the battlefield, and this time Lorkai fought against the thworfs and other creatures that were once in his service.

Zan woke up and threw the sheet aside. He wrapped himself in his cloak and walked outside. The stars shone brightly. Zan arced his head, his mind running over what he had just seen. *Can it be? Can Lorkai be redeemed? It must have just been a dream. Just wishful thinking on my part.* As the wizard tried to reason to himself, he knew that what he had seen was more than a dream. *Was it a premonition? How?*

Zan saw the familiar fog from his dream. Zan surmised that calling it fog was probably inaccurate, for it was a glowing substance that blanketed the land, completely surrounding him and filling him with love and peace.

Zan heard a soft voice whisper, *You saw a possible future. Harkendor may remain as the great enemy, or he may help deliver Goandria from the darkness that has come over it.*

"Who's there?" Zan looked around. "I must be losing my mind."

202

*I am the one who has ordained you as a wizard.*

Zan swallowed hard. "I really am losing my mind," he said quietly. "I need more sleep. All this stress has broken me."

*I have not forgotten you, and you will be delivered from your plight soon. The wizards will fight again, I promise.* The fog faded away, leaving Zan to wonder if he had dreamt it all.

# Flight of the Wizard

# Map of Northern Goandria

# CHAPTER 1

The woman ran down the narrow, dirt road, her brown eyes glancing over her left shoulder. The sky had become splashed with red and violet just over the horizon. A horse neighed distantly behind her, and metal armor clanged. They were coming. She quickly jumped into the woods on the west side of the road and hid behind a tree.

Each breath felt like fire as she panted. The woman pulled her cloak more tightly over her chest, feeling her heart pounding. She sighed deeply and closed her eyes. The clomping of hooves came closer and closer. Her pulse quickened once again. Peering from behind the tree trunk, she saw her hunter: a tall man clad in a brown fur robe with a black hood concealing his face. He abruptly raised his right fist, and the six men following on foot halted. The horseman turned his head, scanning the area.

The woman's mind raced. Could he see her? *My tracks!* she suddenly thought. She drew her sword and whispered as quietly as she could, and the footprints that led to her position disappeared. Still grasping her sword, she ran her left hand along her long, black, braided hair. "Come on, Rina!" she said to herself. "Can't afford to make such rookie mistakes."

The horseman climbed down from his steed. His booted feet landed with a thud. He bent down, surveying the roadway and running a leather-gloved hand over one particular spot. "The trail abruptly ends here," his deep booming voice announced to the others. "Spread out! The mistress received orders from Zontose himself that the wizard must be taken care of." The rest of the men fanned out, only three of them moving toward the forest. As the soldiers looked all around, Rina closed her eyes and attempted to control her breathing. Each thump of her heart seemed to pound louder. The deeper breaths she took, the more she trembled. Her breathing quavered as the soldiers neared her hiding place. *They are going to hear me!* she thought. Now wide-eyed, Rina strained her ears for any sign of movement nearby. However, after several minutes, the soldiers returned to their leader. "There is no sign of the wizard anywhere, commander. It's getting too dark to look for her now," one said.

"She is the only one of her order who is still a real threat to Zontose. Do you wish to explain to him why we came back empty-handed? It will be bad enough telling the katzians the news if we have to," said the commander.

"But she could be anywhere! She has probably used her sorceries to conceal herself by now. We could be standing right on top of her," another soldier chimed in.

Rina's eyes widened, staring into the darkening forest, and then she peeked again from behind the tree trunk. The soldiers had not relented. In spite of their protests, the captain refused to end the search. Dark clouds rolled in from the west, and with them came flurries of snow. Rina pulled her cloak tighter about her. *I need shelter and food if I am to stay out here all night.* Creeping forward, the wizard attempted to scale a slight incline. Her foot slipped, and she let out a scream as she fell backwards into tree.

"There!" a gruff voice called out.

Rina scrambled to get to her feet, but she yelped again, sliding back down to the ground. She gave one more attempt to scurry deeper into the forest, but to no avail. "Where are you going?" a soldier's voice erupted.

"Stay back!" Rina screamed, attempting to raise her sword.

"I don't think so," the commander said from behind her. "You're coming with us."

# CHAPTER 2

Snow continued to fall as the night wore on. The wind howled through the nearby trees, blowing the white powder unrelentingly at the soldiers as they marched onward with their captive. Thick fur and leather protected the men as they plowed on, but Rina was not so lucky. Her clothes did little to hinder the bitter wind, and her hands, which were bound in front of her, had turned purple-blue. The wizard was gagged, and a sword was ever-present behind her as she trudged along. She continually scanned the roadway and outlying forest. *Nothing but white,* she thought to herself.

"How are the thworfs going to meet us in this storm?" A soldier's voice suddenly cut through the wind.

"You would be surprised what their black dragons can accomplish, Polin. You can be certain they are at the fort already," answered the commander.

Dozens of torches popped out against the snow, providing some much welcome light. As the company neared, they spotted glossy, black, stone walls with boxy towers protruding upward. The commander put a horn to his lips, and its deep tone was answered by another from within the fort.

"See? I told you they would be here, Polin."

A meaty hand shoved Rina. "Come on, we haven't got all day."

Rina grunted incoherently, much to the amusement of the men.

"The thworfs won't be as gentle when they get ahold of you!" the soldier cackled.

Rina suddenly fell forward. As her guard came to help her up, she hastily swiped her legs against his ankles, tripping him. Scrambling to her feet, she removed the cloth from her mouth and cried out a slur of words in ancient Goandrian. Her sword leapt from its scabbard around the commander's saddle and landed in her hands before she made off for the forest once again.

"How did this happen?" barked the commander. "After her!"

Behind her, Rina heard the clanking of a gate. Crouching down behind a small snow drift, she cut her hands free as she peered at the fortress. A score of soldiers marched forth, clad in chainmail, leather cloaks, and steel helms that looked like upturned bowls. Their skin was grey, and each of their faces was covered in a brown-black beard. The soldiers were broad shouldered and long limbed but stood no more than five-and-a-half feet tall.

"Thworfs," Polin spat. "Their timing is impeccable as always."

"Find the wizard now, or thworfs will be the least of our concerns!" the commander cried out. Two more soldiers ran off to find Rina. The wind had increased speed, creating a white, snowy fog. It had only been a few minutes since the wizard's escape, but she was once again nowhere to be found.

"Hail Zontose!" a gruff voice called out.

"Hail!" responded the commander.

"Where is the wizard?" the gruff voice asked.

"There have been complications, captain, but she will be back in our hands in a matter of moments. My men are on it as we speak, I assure you."

The thworf snarled and barked orders in a language unintelligible to Rina. "We will find her. Your incompetence is astounding."

Rina did not know where exactly she was heading. All she could see was snow. *I have to get away from the soldiers, but how far have we gotten? How close are they?* To make matters worse, her ankle was screaming in pain and had swollen to the size of her calf. She pressed onward, limping through the piling snow. *This is all too familiar.*

The wind seemed to relent slightly, for off in the distance, Rina thought she saw a small wooden building.

# CHAPTER 3

The thworf's blood-orange eyes strained to see through the blizzard. *She couldn't have gotten far in this blasted weather*, he thought. His steel-studded boots tromped through the ever-deepening snow. He held his sword in his right hand, and the other hand rested on his belt as he slowly moved onward.

"Sir!" a throaty voice called out from in front. "I think we may have found some tracks. It looks like she is heading that way." A gloved hand pointed.

"Do you really think she will help us, captain?" another voice asked.

"I guess we will find out," he answered softly.

They pressed onward until they found a wooden shack, seemingly randomly-placed amongst the woodland. Upon closer inspection, the thworf captain saw only half of it remained. Whether it had been intentionally torn down or nature had its way, he could not say.

Inching around the remaining portion of the structure, the thworf clenched his yellow fangs together, his sword held tightly with both hands now. As he rounded the corner to peek inside, he was greeted by a loud, "Stay back!"

He had found her. The skinny wizard's face was blue and red. She loosely grasped a sword hilt in both hands as she shivered violently. The two stood there, gazes locked, until Rina at last collapsed onto a heap of snow. Her weary eyes remained on the thworf who simply watched her for a moment. "Boys, I found her!"

"You … will … not … take … mmm … eee …" Rina's voice quavered before her eyes closed.

"Quick, gather some wood. She will slip away if she doesn't get warm soon," the captain shouted out to the thworfs.

The captain unclasped his cloak and wrapped it around the wizard. A few minutes later, his soldiers brought wood and started a fire. The flames struggled for life through the wind and snow, but the little shelter the building offered helped just enough to keep it lit.

After an hour passed, Rina finally stirred. "Wha ..." she looked up at the thworfs and immediately pulled away. Breathing heavily, she grasped her weapon again.

"Put that down. You are in no danger from us."

"You are thworfs, the miserable race that invaded our lands. Because of you and your master, I have not had peace! Always on the run ..."

"We aren't what you think, wizard," the captain interrupted. "Those men who were chasing you think we serve Zontose, but we are just a few of a larger force that opposes him. It is true most of my kind gladly submit to the slavery of that man, but there are a few who see through his empty promises."

"But I saw you! I saw you come out of that black fortress!" said Rina.

"They do not know where our true loyalties lie. We are not servants of Zontose, or the Republics for that matter. We simply desire freedom for all races of Goandria," answered the captain.

"None of this makes any sense," Rina said, furrowing her brow as she shifted her gaze to the fire. "If you are no friend to those horrid men, then why did you help them track me down? How do I know this isn't just a ruse? I have never heard of any of your kind that does not see Zontose as a god."

"Nevertheless, there is much I'm sure you haven't heard of, wizard, and alas, here we are. There are more thworfs that oppose Zontose than you realize. The problem is that the vast majority of us are enamored by that man. His sorcery helps keep my people enthralled to him. However, his power is not so great that he can force the unwilling into service."

"Then why pursue me?"

"Because we need someone like you to help overthrow that monster," answered the captain.

"Then you will be disappointed. Since the attack on the Blessed Temples, my powers have been erratic at best. Sometimes I can tap into the blessed power, and other times I can't. I'm not sure why, but I'm seemingly the only one that has any access to magic at all. What hope do you think we could possibly have for success against such impossible numbers?"

"Little by little, we use guerrilla tactics on key locations."

"What is your current target?"

"The nearby fortress," the thworf said with a slight gleam in his eyes.

"Are you insane?" Rina gasped. "I've been trying to get out of here and avoid that place at all costs. What makes you think we have any hope for success?"

The thworf let out a cross between a hiss and a gurgle. "Have you not been paying attention? We won't be attacking head-on. Remember, those men do not know that we are not on their side."

"What is the plan?" Rina asked.

216

"Don't worry about that right now.  You need to rest and regain your strength."

# CHAPTER 4

Rina's eyes slowly opened before going closed again. The wizard pulled a cloak the thworfs gave her closer, and again her eyes reluctantly opened. Above her, a dazzling array of stars gleamed in the clear night sky. Only a few wisps of clouds passed across, reflecting the crescent moon's pale light and adding an exotic texture to the sky. The enjoyment of the night's beauty was short-lived, though, for the cold, bitter wind reminded Rina that it had no plans of going away. "What happened to the fire?" she found herself blurting out drearily, pulling a thick cloak the thworfs gave her closer.

"Why would we want a beacon to alert our enemies to our location?" a deep voice snapped.

Groaning, Rina rolled over and tucked the dual layer of cloaks around her as tight as she could. Her mind slipped into darkness as soon as she had closed her eyes again. It felt like mere seconds before images flashed before her. Hundreds of hooves pounded across the snowy land. She was running, running as long and as hard as she could. Rina headed for a forest, but the trees abruptly vanished. Everywhere she turned, hill, tree, and cave alike disappeared. All that was left was an endless snow-covered wasteland. She could not outrun the horsemen. Fear gripped her. Thoughts of giving up and praying they would be merciful filled her mind. Then she saw them: completely black with metal helmets and masks in the form of snarling creatures. Steadily, the creatures on horseback grew larger and larger. Their swords were twice as tall as they were. They surrounded her, ready to strike, and then her eyes suddenly opened.

Rina sprang up, wide-eyed and panting, realizing she had just woken up from a dream. Her eyes shifted down and noticed the cloaks had been singed. Two spheres of green fire rested in her palms. *What the?* she thought, quickly shaking her hands to extinguish the flames.

"You ... okay?" the captain asked slowly.

Looking up, Rina saw all the thworfs were wide awake and staring at her. "Um," she looked around, eyes wide, searching for some sort of clue. "I uh, I don't know. What happened?"

"I was hoping you could tell us," said the thworf.

"A dream ... there were horse riders. They were chasing me. No matter where I went, I could not escape, and just when they were about to strike, I woke up." She rubbed her temple.

"So this is because of a nightmare?" The thworf furrowed his brow, slowly walking over to the woman. She had burns on her legs and hands. Her clothes had holes burned right through them, and the cloaks were now a blackened and tattered mess. Clawed fingers gently ran along he charred cloaks. "Have your powers manifested like this before when you had a bad dream?"

Rina shook her head.

The thworf's nostrils flared, taking a couple whiffs. He grabbed the top cloak and pressed it against his face. "Strange, it doesn't smell burnt. It smells *sweet.*" He sniffed it again. "Yes, definitely sweet."

"Do you know why?" Rina asked.

"No."

"I don't know what is going on," the wizard sighed, placing her hands over her face. "Everything is just … I can't do this anymore. I have nowhere to turn, and everywhere I go, I am hunted. If I can make it to the Republics, maybe things will be different. I need to return to the Blessed Temples and try to see what happened."

The thworf gently rested a hand on her arm. "It won't matter."

Rina's face tightened, and her head twitched back. "Why do you say that? Who are you to try to determine my fate? I hardly know you, and I'm fairly positive you are not much different than the rest of your kind. I never knew of any thworf that wasn't bent on destroying the world."

"I already addressed that," the captain said coolly.

"I do not know if anything you say is true. What I do know is that your people and their allies have been chasing me for months. I have never been able to stay in one location long. I cannot stay in a village or inn due to the bounty, and for all I know, this is some elaborate trick to finally trap me." Tears streaked her face as she spoke. "And now this …"

"Tharakk. My name is Tharakk," the thworf said, running his thumb and forefinger over his chin hair.

"Huh?"

"I never told you my name, and if I would like you to trust me, I feel that is a good place to start."

"Indeed." Rina sighed. "It is probably best if we all get some sleep and talk more about all this in the morning." With that, she rolled over and closed her eyes, hoping the thworf would let her be. But she was nowhere near sleeping. Once the thworfs had all laid down or otherwise minded their own business, her eyes opened again. Before her was an area about a foot in diameter where the snow had thinned, and within it was a cluster of brown weeds. The jagged-edged plants lay pressed into the earth, wilted and forgotten. In months past, they had sprouted small burgundy flowers with bristling petals, slightly resembling a clover. In the spring, these weeds grew all over the northern region of Goandria, peppering dark crimson amongst the fresh green foliage. *Now you are forgotten. Perhaps your existence was never known. Maybe that is the fate of the Republics and of the wizards themselves,* she thought.

# CHAPTER 5

Tharakk opened his eyes. The sun had already risen, yet a grayness hung overhead. Light rain beat down on his face, and distant rumblings sounded. Getting up, he stretched and slowly collected his belongings. What was once snow had become a soupy mess of icy mud amongst the snowdrifts. "A thunderstorm? But there was a blizzard a couple days ago." He shook his head. The temperature was a bit warmer, but not by much. The wind still howled, making the rain feel even colder than the snow from the other day.

"Captain!" a thworf saluted as the officer walked by. His comrades were bustling about. Some were attempting to get a fire started in a desperate hope to get warm. Others were talking and munching on dried fruit, and Rina was still fast asleep.

"How is she, Irin?" Tharakk asked a soldier who was crushing leaves in a bowl and applying the concoction to Rina's burns.

"It's difficult to say, sir. It's probable you may have to forego your plans of attacking the fortress. Or we might have to do it without her. Things will get even worse if we don't get her out of this cold."

*One thing after another,* he thought bitterly, chewing on the inside of his cheek while he watched Irin spread more herbs on her injuries.

"What is our next move, captain? We can't stay here."

"Remember when she awoke and I said I smelled something sweet? Did you smell it too?" Tharakk asked.

"Yes, faintly."

"Why would something burnt smell sweet?"

Irin shrugged. "It may have something to do with her magic, but you didn't answer my question. What are your orders?"

"I cannot shake the feeling that the scent is a clue."

Irin rolled his eyes but humored his captain. "A clue to what?"

"That is the mystery," Tharakk trailed off, pacing back and forth and fingering his beard and grey lips. "What if Rina has the ability to heal herself?" he said mostly to himself, now eyeing the sleeping wizard.

"Before the attack on the Blessed Temples it would have been possible to some degree, but now ... Nothing is certain. She said herself that her powers are erratic."

"Sir," a tall thworf interrupted. One hand held a bow as the other mindlessly caressed his sword pommel. "How long are we going to wait around like this? We need to hit the fortress before another blizzard comes." A few thworfs grunted in agreement.

"The wizard is injured, and she is the cornerstone of my plan. You all need to be patient," Tharakk said calmly.

"Looks like the plan has changed, Captain," another interjected.

"Yeah! We are just sittin' ducks out here. How long do ya think it'll be before the men of Dalarashess realize we aren't their allies?" said yet another one.

Tharakk combed his fingers through his chin hairs again. "Hmm, that's true, but the odds are against us if we go in without her."

"Uhh," Rina groaned, stretching her arms outward. "Wha- what … where am I?" She startled awake.

"It's okay, calm down," Irin said gently.

"Thworfs?" She jumped, quickly feeling for her weapon. A dark emerald aura began to form around the wizard. Her wide eyes staring at the thworfs while she hastily searched for her sword. Gritting her teeth, Rina frantically threw the cloaks aside, patting the area. "Where is it? Where did you put it, you snakes?"

"Tharakk, look at her eyes," Irin whispered to the captain.

"They're … green … What do you suppose that means?"

"I don't know, but it also looks like whatever is going on has caused her wounds to heal too."

Tharakk's eyes scanned the areas where Rina's legs were burned. Other than charred and tattered clothing, there was absolutely no sign of last night's incident. "Look at her. She doesn't seem to know where she is. She could be living out a dream."

"I would say that is probably true, since she was the one who last held her sword."

As Tharakk and Irin spoke to one another, the captain's feet moved back slightly, and he kept his focus on the wizard. His blood felt like hot liquor coursing through his veins, and his grey skin took on a slight green coloration. Then, looking down with one eye narrowed a bit, his feet halted, fearing what might be going on.

"Her powers are sapping all the energy around her!" Tharakk gagged.

"Wizards cannot do that! It is in direct violation of the laws of wizard magic," the other protested.

"Wake her! Wake her now!"

Irin shook Rina, but his attempts at waking her failed. "It must be Zontose's tampering with the wizards' powers."

"You need to wake her now!" Tharakk coughed, clutching his throat as he fell to his knees. His vision faded and colors swirled. He felt like his life would soon be forfeit, but then air filled his lungs again, and what had taken hold suddenly stopped. Rina had awoken.

The wizard wrinkled her brow and noticed the panting thworf captain. "Did something happen again?"

"I would say so! You nearly killed me!" Tharakk snarled.

"What?" Rina gasped.

"Captain, do you remember when we were stationed in Morhelgol and Zontose would sneak off to the lowest depths of the fortress? When he emerged, he was always stronger. It was then that he would sometimes punish those he felt were insubordinate by draining their life. I saw it happen once from a distance, but it isn't something I could easily forget. I wonder if what he did to the wizard temples altered her powers, leaving a sort of impression on them. We both know that Zontose is a sorcerer, but what he wields is not wizard magic," Irin said.

"I wish I knew what is going on!" Rina interjected. "I pray that your theory is wrong."

"Me too," said Irin. "But we must consider that whatever the source of your plight is, it is not something Zontose will expect us to use against him."

"Wait, don't I have any say in this? Something is seriously wrong, and I need to get back to the Blessed Temples as soon as I can," Rina said.

"Then what?" asked Tharakk. "If you make it back to the temples, how will that solve your problem? The wizards' powers are removed. All you would do is pose a danger to your comrades. Wouldn't you prefer to find a way to understand what is going on and use it against Zontose?"

"Well, yes, and that is exactly why I want to go back to the temples. I cannot help you in the way you want me to. I am dangerous to be around."

"That's not what I mean. Maybe you could try to train yourself to focus and relearn your abilities," said Tharakk.

"It might work. In truth, we do not know what is happening to you either. It was a suggestion, nothing more," Irin added.

# CHAPTER 6

The wicker basket exploded. Green flames continued to lick the ends of the pieces that now lay strewn about the ground. Rina sighed and stomped over to where the basket had been. She placed a new one on the stump. "It doesn't get any better! My magic is more sporadic than it ever has been!"

"I think you can do it. It might take longer than you thought, but you'll get there." Tharakk feigned a smile through the worry lines on his face.

"She is right, though," Irin whispered in his ear. "She isn't getting ahold of her powers. This is taking way too long."

"Haven't you been the one pushing me to be more patient over the last week?" Tharakk asked with a wry smile.

Irin breathed out through his wide nose and looked up at his commander. "Yes, but I'm starting to have doubts. There is no improvement, and I'm starting to feel like it may never happen." Another basket's life ended in flames. "See?"

"Maybe she cannot do this alone. Perhaps another wizard could help her, but we both know none of them have powers except Rina."

The basket lifted about three feet and sat back down without exploding. "Wait, did you see that?" Tharakk exclaimed.

"No, I didn't. Did she do it?" Irin said cynically.

"Look, it happened again!" Tharakk pointed. "Rina! Can you try to do that with something heavier this time? How about that pile of weapons?" he called out to the wizard.

Rina waved in acknowledgement. The weapons levitated, separated according to size, and were neatly placed back down. Tharakk ran over to her, his eyes wide as he looked at her then back at the weapons. "How? How did you learn to do that so quickly?"

"I don't know if I would say *quickly*," Irin snorted.

"Don't get too confident in what I can do yet. It may be temporary, but I felt some sort of shift in the magical currents. The best way I can describe it is if you start out sailing on a rough sea amidst a storm. After days of that, the storm subsides and the currents settle down. Even though things feel calmer, there is still a faint darkness somewhere. It feels powerful, but very distant. I have neither experienced anything like this before, nor read about it in the library at the Temples."

"This all seemingly happened just now?" Irin asked, skepticism heavy in his voice.

Rina shrugged. "Yes, it appears so, but I do not know how long it will last."

"So the problem isn't with you. It is the magic." Tharakk sighed. "If it continues to be this sporadic, it could be a problem."

"It might not be entirely the magic. It could be the way the magic and I interact. Being a wizard means a mutual relationship with the blessed powers."

"Horses," Irin whispered, lifting his nose upward. "I smell horses. We need to get the others up and moving. The northmen are coming!"

"I don't smell anything," Tharakk protested.

"It's probably because of your age, captain." Irin smirked.

"Careful," Tharakk playfully jabbed the other. "Yes, I smell them now. Humans have such a *distinct* stench," the captain said carefully, looking at Rina. "They are moving fast; I can hear their hooves. Pick up your things, men! We need to move now!"

The other thworfs scurried about the camp. It wasn't long before arrows whizzed through the leaves and stuck into the ground near the troops. One thworf already had an arrow through his left thigh.

"Why are they attacking us?" one of the soldiers blurted before an arrow went through his skull.

Five fur-clad men emerged from behind a few trees, charging at the thworfs with broad double-headed axes. The thworfs charged at their new foes and formed into an attack stance. Snow and mud flew up behind a brown warhorse. Rina ducked down when she saw the rider. Her eyes widened as she watched him carve through several thworfs. Tharakk's company pulled back, still locked in formation with spearmen in the front and swordsmen in the back. A moment later, the thworf captain stormed up to the horseman with Irin trailing by his side.

*The commander. How did he find us here, and why is he attacking us? For all he knows, the thworfs are allies of his ... Unless ...* Rina thought in a panic as she watched the skirmish unfold.

"What is the meaning of this? Once Morhelgol gets word that you attacked one of its squads, you will all be executed!"

"There most definitely will be executions, Tharakk, but I will certainly not be among them," the commander scoffed. "You can surrender and die later, or fight to the last man. It makes little difference to me, and the fact that you invoke Morhelgol's power and name is amusing, traitor!"

"How dare you hurl such accusations at me! What proof do you have?"

"You are harboring an enemy of the Dalarashess Empire," the commander said matter-of-factly. "Perhaps if you admit your treachery and hand her over now, Lord Zontose will grant you and your comrades mercy."

"I have done no such thing," Tharakk replied coolly.

The commander smiled thinly. "Indeed. So, you are sticking by your tale of innocence? Then my scouts who have been watching you nurture and aid the wizard are liars?"

Tharakk remained quiet, but his eyes shifted to Irin briefly, causing the commander to sneer with delight. "Come now. You are not going to officially accuse my men of being liars to my face? Where is that bravado you were displaying a little bit ago? Come on, Tharakk, I want to see it again, once more, before I kill you. No? Very well then, I guess that is all the enjoyment I will have for one day."

Tharakk bit his tongue and glowered at the commander, and his soldiers held their positions, unwilling to relent.

"You're outnumbered. Is one wizard really worth it?" The commander's mouth twisted into a cruel smile.

"Yes," Tharakk hissed through clenched teeth, "because everyone who willingly follows that monster is a traitor to Goandria! Zontose declares himself a god and enslaves those who serve him instead of freeing them as he promised. My people are dying in masses for his cause, and he could hardly care. Zontose will burn, and so will you!"

Rina watched, crouched and hidden. Her jaw clenched and her eyes rarely blinked. Sweat began to bead on her forehead in spite of the cold. She mumbled something under her breath and lifted her fingers outward toward the northmen. The snow before the commander's horse exploded upward, causing the steed to rear back in fright. Rina took advantage of the distraction and threw a blast of orange fire at the men. The thworfs raised their shields over their faces as their burning enemies shrieked and howled.

"Find her!" the commander barked. Four soldiers fanned out toward the tree line but were greeted by more balls of fire. One of the soldiers near the commander placed a horn to his lips. The instrument echoed with a shrill tone, causing Rina's ears to ring as if a gong was continually beaten within her head. Crouching on her stomach, Rina crawled behind a different tree five paces to her left. She raised her left hand, and green lightning streamed from her fingertips, searing through a northman from behind.

"She's toying with us!" a man shouted to the commander just before a fire ball consumed him as well. The thworfs moved in, slicing through the men of Dalarashess. Thworf swords fluidly sliced through armor and flesh, never ceasing, never slowing, and never breaking formation. The commander of the northmen clutched his oozing thigh as he slid backward. "Traitors," he growled through clenched teeth. "You will all die! Every last one of you!" Explosions of snow and dirt and screams of agony and death permeated the area.

Off in the distance, armor and footsteps clamored. A few minutes later, more arrows whirred through the air at the thworfs. "They have reinforcements!" Tharakk barked to his men who instantly stepped back but still held firm.

Rina came out from the shadows, arms down with palms facing forward. The hood of her cloak concealed most of her face, save for a faint reflection of her cold eyes. Two northmen were lifted into the air by unseen forces and abruptly slammed together. Seven more ran toward her, only to be fried by a barrage of green lightning.

"Ignore the traitors! Focus on the wizard!" The commander shouted. Suddenly, dozens of men marched from the depths of the forest, converging on the wizard's location.

"To Rina!" Tharakk commanded, and the thworfs moved in unison toward her, cutting down enemies along the way, but as instructed, the northmen paid them little mind. They outnumbered the thworfs at least seven to one and relied on that to keep pushing forward.

*What is Rina thinking? She isn't strong enough to take them all by herself. She could hardly control her powers mere days ago!* Tharakk thought. Panting through the visor of his helm, he glanced over at Irin, who seemed to be wearing the same expression: furrowed brow, hardened eyes, and pursed lips.

"She is going to get herself killed," Irin breathed.

"Pray that a miracle happens," Tharakk replied through clenched teeth.

# CHAPTER 7

"We need to get out of here, or we will all die. There are too many of them, Tharakk," Irin whispered to the captain.

"I know, but we aren't abandoning Rina."

"I didn't suggest that we should, but the northmen keep coming. If we don't act now, we will be annihilated."

"How do you suggest we get Rina out of that mess? Look at all of them! Our warriors can hold their own but not against that!"

"I don't know, but we either have to do act now or retreat."

"We have to try. Keep your voice down!" Tharakk snapped. *We are going to get out of this. With Rina.* He bore his teeth and signaled his men to push on toward the wizard. Waves of men came at Rina, their weapons moving with short but fluid motions, but Rina managed to dodge away from each attack. Several men of Dalarashess flew backward, others became victims of lightning or fire, but through all this, Rina remained unscathed. Arrows stopped short of striking the wizard and fell to the ground in heaps. Rina's eyes turned deep green, splashed with a hint of white. As Tharakk drew closer to her, he realized that her eyes hadn't changed color; fire was coming from the edges of her eyelids. The longer she fought, the more the thworf noticed the fire, and it soon appeared that her eyes had morphed completely into green flames. Soon, there was so much energy radiating out of Rina's body that her skin also had a green tint to it.

234

Magical tendrils and fireballs exploded from the wizard's hands without even a moment's pause. Rina's hands moved so quickly they were no more than a blur to those around her. It looked to Tharakk that she was some sort of magical automaton constructed solely for the purpose of fighting. *What are we actually doing to help? How can my men help when she wields such power?* the captain thought. As his men attacked the rear flank, the northmen only fought back when they had no choice but to defend their own lives.

Then, with what sounded like thunder, there was a magical burst from Rina's position, hurling waves of energy outward, knocking everyone onto their backs. Tharakk's head spun. He tried to get up only to fall back down. His ears rang with such intensity that he felt like his head was going to explode. Cradling his temples, Tharakk shook his head. The world spun around him, and he threw up when he attempted to stand again.

Each minute felt like an hour as Tharakk lay there, disoriented and unable to gain his bearings. Some time later, he heard Irin through the haze. Reopening his eyes, Tharakk saw the thworf and Rina hovering over him.

"You need to stand up, now!" Rina's soft voice shouted.

Tharakk moaned inaudibly as the wizard and thworf helped the captain to his feet. "How are you two standing?" He groaned.

"Sheer will," Irin said cheekily through a sideways grin.

"The others?" Tharakk asked, as Irin and Rina pulled him to his feet.

"Most are safe. We thworfs are hardier than those humans, but we lost a few in the confusion."

"Rina, what did you do?"

The wizard didn't reply, but instead continued to help the thworfs to their feet. Eventually Tharakk's vision cleared, and the ringing in his ears subsided. His eyes surveyed the area. The northmen were strewn about the ground. "Rina, what happened? How did you kill all of them?"

"They aren't all dead, but many are," she said soberly.

"How?" Tharakk swallowed hard, still staring at the ground.

Rina and Tharakk locked eyes briefly before looking away abruptly. "I wish I could tell you. I don't remember much. I was fighting, and I could feel the magical currents flowing through me like they never have before. Then everyone was on the ground, and I couldn't use magic again."

Tharakk sighed. "The men of Dalarashess are on to us, and you have lost your magic again. An attack on their fortress seems out of the question."

"Let's not get ahead of ourselves," Irin said as the thworf soldiers limped their way deeper into the nearby woods.

An hour later, the company of thworfs made camp to take a rest. Tharakk took a seat on a large stone and placed his face in the palms of his hands. "We should be far enough away from those men by now, but we probably shouldn't risk a fire."

"Our men will freeze if we don't," Irin countered.

236

The captain exhaled loudly. "Fine, but we can't risk being spotted. Rina! Come over here."

"Yes, captain?" the wizard asked.

Tharakk flinched briefly at hearing her address him by his title, but his hard expression returned in seconds. "You have to tell me what happened out there. Your magic nearly killed my men, and it left us all very weak and sick. I don't want to hear something along the lines of 'I don't know.' If me and my men are going to accompany you, we need to know what we are getting into."

"I want to know just as much as you do," Rina shrugged, silently hoping that the thworf wouldn't press the matter.

"Rina, you know that isn't good enough."

The wizard's eyebrows met in the center, and her right eyelid narrowed as she chewed her bottom lip. "My magic is still unstable. I thought it smoothed out, but during the fight, I felt it intensify more than ever." As she spoke, Tharakk's eyes met her hands which had red and black blotches on the skin that looked like a cross between a rash and a burn.

Seeing where Tharakk was looking, Rina quickly hid her hands within the sleeves of her cloak. "It's fine. It will be healed tomorrow or the day after."

"That's pretty optimistic, don't you think? Those are pretty severe wounds."

"It's magical backlash. It happens from time to time when too much magic is used, and like I said, that was the most magic I ever tapped into."

"When do you think your magic will return? I sure hope it won't take weeks again for it to stabilize. My

237

men are tough, but we won't be able to take the fortress without you and your magic."

"I know. I will do what I can to make sure my magic returns quickly and won't endanger your men."

# CHAPTER 8

Two small fires hungrily ate away at a clump of logs. Few words were spoken amongst the relaxing company, and Rina took a moment to sneak off alone. Looking behind her, it seemed to the wizard that no one noticed she had left. She reached two trees that jettisoned out of the ground. Stopping just a few feet from the trees, Rina reached out her left hand and rubbed a leaf between her thumb and forefinger. Taking in a sharp inhale then slowly breathing out from her nose, Rina closed her eyes, and the leaf slowly began to glow with a red sheen. When her eyes opened, the leaf glowed brighter for a short moment then became dark once again. *What will it take? Why is this happening? I wish I could go back to the Blessed Temples. There has to be something wrong there.*

Rina plucked the leaf off its stem and let it rest in her palm. Her eyes narrowed as she focused on the leaf, and it burst into green flames before crumbling to ash. *Is my magic back already? That doesn't make any sense.* This time she pointed toward a low hanging branch and dipped her finger downward. The branch followed suit. *I have access to magic again, but is it stable? Maybe it's too risky to rely on magic too much. Next time, the thworfs or I might not survive.*

"It looks like everything is in order, Rina," Irin popped up out of the darkness.

"So it seems."

"You don't sound very convinced."

"I think you will have to agree that I have every reason to be cautious. I nearly killed all of you."

"But you didn't kill us, so there is no need to be so hard on yourself."

"Yes, yes there is! I felt controlled by my magic, and that shouldn't be possible for a wizard. A wizard tapping that much into the blessed power should be cut off forever, but I'm not. What's scary is that if we attack the fortress, it may happen again. There are a lot of soldiers there, and I will have to utilize so much of the blessed power that I don't know what will happen."

"Tharakk knows. He may not say it, but he knows. None of us really expected to live to see Zontose overthrown or the end of the war. What we expect is to die fighting on the right side, not in slavery to a madman. In answer to the question on your mind, yes, we are willing to risk our lives and die if that is needed. Your magic, reliable or not, is the key to our success. It is why Tharakk wanted you to join us."

Rina smiled. "You know, it is still difficult for me to believe I am allies with thworfs. Tharakk implied earlier that there are others out there, but I haven't seen or heard of thworfs taking up arms against Zontose as you guys have."

Irin sighed. "Before I came up here, I spoke to Tharakk. He wants to move the attack on the fortress to the day after tomorrow."

"Are you serious? So soon?" Rina's voice shrieked.

"Yes, it appears our captain wants to move in whether or not you, or the rest of us, are ready."

"Do you think that is a good idea? To mount an attack so soon would require non-stop traveling from tomorrow morning until we arrive."

Irin looked away and ground his heel into the mud. "It isn't my place to agree or disagree with such things. If the captain wants my opinion, I offer it. Otherwise it is his decision on when and what we do."

"I don't feel comfortable with this plan at all. It's reckless and borderline suicidal," Rina protested.

"I understand your concerns, but I've served with Tharakk a long time. If he makes a decision, it doesn't come lightly."

"I don't know. It sounds to me like he simply wants his revenge. Did he tell you his plans for attacking the fortress? It obviously isn't something we can do by sheer force. We don't have the numbers," Rina said, suspicion laden in her voice.

"No, he just said that he plans to start the trek in four hours."

"Four hours!" Rina gasped.

Irin nodded with a grim half-smile on his face. "There is a lot to prepare for, friend. Your magic is one of them. I don't want to put any more pressure on you, but it wouldn't be a bad idea to spend that time working on understanding your magic better."

"My understanding is just fine. The problem lies with the fundamentals of the magic itself. There is a hindrance, a sort of damper on it, that sometimes comes off and unleashes a torrent of magic before it closes again."

"Is there any way to predict when this occurs?" Irin asked, although privately he already suspected the answer.

Rina shook her head. "If there is, I haven't found it yet."

Irin grunted under his breath, looked over his shoulder one last time as he made the first few steps to walk off, then disappeared down into the campsite.

# CHAPTER 9

The beams of light arched right into Rina's eyes, wrestling her from the snoring that gripped her merely seconds prior. The cool wind tossed her hair about gently, and the sound of water running told the wizard that warmer weather was upon them. She instinctively placed her hands on the ground to lift herself up, only to sink into muck up to her wrists. "Ugh," Rina grumbled, flicking the mud and snow off her hands. She wiped the rest off with her cloak then stretched her muscles and reattempted to stand up with the help of a nearby tree. *I feel like I got hit in the head with an axe*, she thought, clumsily walking down the hillside to the thworf camp.

All thworfs were standing in formation, making Rina feel like it was some sort of welcoming party for her. "Hello?" She yawned awkwardly.

"It's time, Rina. Are you ready?" Tharakk asked coldly.

"Yes, I, I think so."

"You *think* you are?"

"No, no, I am." She unleashed another yawn.

"You don't look it, Rina, and we are going to depend on you out there if things go awry. Can we do that?" Tharakk pressed.

"Sure, sorry, my head …" Rina mumbled, and that was the last thing she remembered.

Once again, bright rays of light were the first things to greet Rina when she opened her eyes. The next thing she noticed was branches of evergreens slowly passing her by. The wizard's face wrinkled in confusion as she gawked at her surroundings. She was lying on her back being dragged along on stretcher of sorts. Firmly patting her hands on the crude contraption told her it was no more than a few spare cloaks tied to two long branches.

"She's awake!" A thworf shouted. Suddenly the trees stopped moving.

Rina took several deep breaths. Her head no longer swam, and the fatigue she felt earlier had almost completely subsided. "Are you feeling better?" Rina heard Irin's voice say.

"Yes, how long have you been carrying me?"

"Nearly two days."

"Two days! What happened, why was I unconscious for so long?"

"We don't know. You abruptly collapsed, and we couldn't wake you," Irin replied.

Rina spun her legs around and stood up, wobbling a little before straightening up. "If I've lost that much time, that means we are almost at the fortress!"

"We will arrive probably tomorrow. Your *situation* slowed us down considerably," remarked one of the thworfs who had been carrying the makeshift stretcher.

"Why did you take me with, then?" Rina asked, immediately realizing it was a stupid question.

"We don't leave people behind to die," Tharakk's voice echoed. "It would completely go against everything we fight for if we left you unconscious in the wilderness."

"I don't expect you to delay your plans on my behalf."

"We did. Now that you are feeling better, we needn't delay any further." Tharakk signaled the thworfs to continue their march.

Snow started to gently sail down from the sky an hour later. As the band moved northward, the evergreen branches hung lower and closer together. Rina noticed that the spacing between the trees had rapidly diminished. The forest became so dense that Tharakk and two other thworfs had to hack a path with their weapons. The snow that fell was slushy, as if it couldn't decide if it wanted to be rain, snow, or both. It soaked Rina and the thworfs through every layer of clothing until they were all shivering furiously.

A couple of crows cawed off to the west, startling Rina. She instinctively reached for her weapon. A nearby thworf noticed and smirked, shaking his head a little, but he kept any thoughts to himself.

The soggy march felt like it would never end for Rina. For short moments, the wizard would get lost in her thoughts, then notice that the sun had hardly moved and there was still plenty of daylight left. *How far have we gone? A mile? Two miles? Three? It is so hard to tell, and moving in this stuff isn't easy. It feels like we aren't gaining any ground at all. It's so depressing and cold. The sky is grey as far as I can see. And all this blasted snow! My hair is wet, my cloak is soaked, and I can't stop shivering.* Rina sighed. *I should be grateful, I guess. Tharakk could have easily left me, and he would have been justified in doing so. He owes me nothing. The thworfs are a little rough sometimes, but they are alright. I wish the rest of Goandria knew there were thworfs out there who don't worship Zontose.*

"We stop here for now. You will all need your rest. Tomorrow we attack," Tharakk called out over his shoulder.

Rina sat down on a nearby tree stump, running her hands over her forearms, but nothing could keep her shivering at bay. Within minutes the thworfs had a fire crackling. *How do they do that when it's so wet?* She wondered, practically running toward the heat.

She reached her hands over the fire. The warmth was so refreshing, but it seemed foreign to her tired and cold muscles, causing them to ache even more.

"How much further? I don't recognize where we are," Rina said.

"We are less than a mile east of the stronghold," Irin replied.

"That's it? I thought we were further than that," Rina remarked.

"No, there is a reason we trudged through here. It bypasses the roadway. The northmen rarely come this way, and if they do, it would be in small enough numbers to handle," Tharakk chimed in. "We attack at night. Everyone, try to get some sleep if you can."

# CHAPTER 10

Rina lay down and tried to get comfortable. Despite the large fire and the heat it radiated, the wizard still felt cold and wet. Rina dug the snow from the area with her hands, but the damp mud just soaked through her clothes. Sighing loudly, she readjusted onto her back and the sinking ooze slowly devoured her hair, legs, and arms. After a few minutes of trying to ignore the discomfort, she got up. Throwing off her cloak she rubbed it in the snow, scrubbing as much of the mud and clay out as possible, then held it near the fire to dry.

A couple thworfs were already snoring loudly, and the rest were curled up peacefully, seemingly unbothered by the less than ideal sleeping conditions. One of Tharakk's men stoically stood watch, his sword drawn.

*He stands so still,* Rina thought, *he could easily be mistaken for a statue.* She smiled a little at the thought then sighed. *I slept for two days, and that is enough. If only I knew how to pass the time until the sun sets. Wonder how they sleep so soundly in the muck? Looking at them, it seems like these thworfs couldn't tell the difference between an inn bed and this nasty ground.*

As the minutes slowly passed to hours, Rina sparked a small magical fireball in her right hand and passed it back and forth from one hand to the other. Her eyes shifted to her cloak, which was now mostly brown instead of blue. She smoothed the back of it over her legs and hovered her hand over the material. The wizard closed her eyes, and a white light streamed from her palms. Small flakes of mud pulled away from the fabric and dissolved as they touched the beam of light. Opening her eyes, Rina let out her breath and slumped in frustration. *That isn't working very well. It will take days at this rate. All I can do is hope that the cloak is dry enough to use by the time the thworfs get up.*

Once Rina could feel her toes again, she wandered off toward a tree stump. Sitting on it, she folded her arms across her chest and leaned forward. Closing her eyes, she let herself slowly slip into slumber.

The next thing Rina knew, she was running. Large lupine creatures trampled after her on all fours with blazing eyes of red fire. She ran as fast as she could, but it didn't matter. The beasts were gaining ground quickly. Teeth protruded from their jaws like daggers, and saliva dripped from them. The creatures' eyes bore right through her. Rina managed a quick look over her shoulder, but it was too late. An open maw filled with razor teeth was the last thing she saw before her eyes opened.

Despite the cool air, the wizard's body and forehead were covered in sweat, amplifying the cold. Goosebumps formed along her arms and legs, and a violent shiver gripped her. It wasn't long before Rina noticed the sun's potency had dimmed as it grew close to the horizon. Then she saw Tharakk, watching her with a grin creasing his face.

"It's good to see you got some rest. We will make our attack soon."

"How do you think we will take the entire stronghold ourselves?" Rina asked.

A nearby thworf grunted as he rolled over in his sleep. "As we always do: distraction and stealth. Up and at 'em, boys!" Tharakk shouted, slapping the back of one of his sleeping soldiers. "It's time!" Then facing Rina again, the captain said, "It won't be easy, and our success largely depends on you, but for now, let's just focus on getting to the fort."

Nearly an hour and a half later, the old, right-angled fort revealed itself against the snow. Frost and ice lined the outer wall, and a half dozen sentries paced back and forth mechanically.

"Rina, do you see that wagon of hay? Can you light it on fire?" Tharakk asked.

"I can try." Rina flexed her hand muscles and tossed a green orb of fire at the hay. The wagon and its contents were instantly ablaze. A bell in the central tower screamed, and horns echoed throughout the fortress.

"Now, spread out into the wilderness behind the fort. Take cover anywhere you can find it," Tharakk ordered.

The thworfs fanned out, ducking behind trees or snowbanks. Rina followed Tharakk as he and Irin positioned themselves behind a snowdrift. Three minutes later, the heavy gates of the fortress groaned open, and four squads marched forth. Swordsmen with their weapons in hand were at the front, and archers notched arrows to their bowstrings in the rear. As the Northmen mobilized troops on the ground, archers lined the wall, arrows ready to fly at a moment's notice. However, the back side of the fort, where the thworfs hid, had very few sentries. A few pikemen stalked the tops of the towers, but it was obvious that they didn't prioritize guarding that side of the fort. Tharakk waved his left hand, and a thworf pulled out his bow. Crouching as he stepped out from behind a tree, he shot one of the pikemen between the eyes. Just as one of the other sentries ran over to see what happened, he too fell victim to a thworf arrow.

Again, Tharakk signaled with his left hand, and two more thworfs ran up to the base of the fortress wall with a load of kindling.

"Now it's your turn." The captain clasped Rina's shoulder.

Nodding, Rina shot a ball of fire at the pile of wood. Green flames mushroomed outward. The men of Dalarashess ran over to flaming wood. Some of them were picked off by arrows, and the thworfs dispersed again before anyone could see them.

"They're playing with us!" One of the men barked, slashing the fire with his sword a few times before signaling a group of soldiers to follow him. He was a stout man compared to his comrades, but he had a bulky muscular frame and didn't wear a helmet like the others. His long red hair and beard blazed like fire. A deep scar ran from the top right of his hair line to the lower left corner of his jaw, making him look even more angry as he searched for the attackers. After about twenty paces or so, the red haired officer stopped in a small clearing and raised his left fist. The men trailing behind halted. Without warning, a volley of arrows peppered the northmen from the tree tops, killing all of them in seconds. Rina darted through the fallen men and scampered up a pine as quickly as she could. Clinging on as tightly as she could, Rina snuck a peek at the ground, and she clung closer to the trunk. More men of Dalarashess came to investigate their fallen comrades only to be met with arrows flying at them as well. Rina hesitantly peeled her left hand from the tree, and shakily tried to get a spell out, but before the fire could manifest, she felt her other hand slip. As Rina repositioned herself, the group of northmen were all killed by thworf arrows.

Five thworfs, led by Irin, scaled the jagged, irregular stones that made up the fortress' defensive wall, using only their claws to make the ascent. Rina, watched in amazement as Irin and the others quickly made the climb without tools or ropes to aid them. Once they were on top of the wall, Rina followed Tharakk down from the pine, the large needles pricking her with every move she made. The wizard glanced down and saw that Tharakk and the thworfs had already reached the ground. She still had a quarter of the tree left to go, struggling to find footing with each step downward.

"Rina! Are you coming?" Tharakk breathed loudly.

"Yes! I'm just..." Her voice cracked, and her foot slipped off a branch. Rina landed on her back in the pine needles.

Laughing, Tharakk reached out and helped the wizard to her feet. "That was graceful," he chuckled, shaking his head.

Rina's face flushed, but she held her tongue. "What do we do now?" She asked, hoping the change of subject would diminish her embarrassment.

"Now we wait for Irin."

Keeping low, Rina, Tharakk, and the rest of the thworfs hid themselves, breathlessly waiting. Rina looked at Tharakk, who watched the fort like a dragon stalking its prey. *What are we waiting for? Irin isn't going to take the fort himself. How much longer do we have to hide before we can do something? My heart is pounding, and I can't take much more of this excitement! Ugh, it feels like we have been waiting for an hour, but it's probably only been about fifteen minutes or so. How do they stay so still for so long? I don't think Tharakk has moved at all since he said we need to wait for Irin.* While these thoughts swirled in Rina's head, a slight movement in the right corner tower caught her eye. The wizard refocused her attention to that spot, and a second later, fire burst from the tower, hurling stone and debris outward. Then another blast occurred at the base of the tower, causing the ground to quake beneath Rina. There was a half-minute of peace; everything was still in that briefest of moments. Northmen rushed to the tower to investigate, but as soon as those few seconds had passed, the tower crumbled. The men of Dalarashess fled in terror, but most were crushed or trapped beneath huge chunks of stone.

Tharakk nodded to everyone else. Unsheathing their swords, they leapt out, running toward the northmen in a triangle formation, cutting down their foes like a scythe. The thworfs maintained their pace, plowing right through the northmen's defenses straight into the gaping hole in the wall. Corpses were strewn periodically in the halls, and the faint sound of steel clashing against steel rang in the background.

*It looks like the thworfs are doing a fine job without me. I wonder why they think they need me so much.* Rina thought, gazing at the destruction the thworfs left. It was a terrible sight for the wizard to behold. Soldiers, gutted and bloody, littered the fort, and some still wore their final expressions. Intellectually, Rina knew they were the enemy, and in war, death is the natural result, but her heart was deeply affected by the sights around her.

252

Rina and the thworfs marched down the empty corridors of the fortress until they reached a courtyard in the center. There, Irin and his men met up with the rest of the thworfs. Rina noticed they were three thworfs short, and she knew Krifae, Belnor, and Rifel had met their fate. She swallowed a large lump in her throat as the blood-stained thworfs made their report to Tharakk.

"Rina, are you ready?" Tharakk's deep voice echoed.

"Ready for what exactly? You guys already did most of the work. The fortress is taken."

Tharakk loosed another hearty laugh. "Not by a long shot, wizard. The true fight is about to begin. This was only the warm-up."

A deep rumble vibrated the atmosphere. Rina's eyes shot upward as a stream of fire arced overhead.

"The cavalry has arrived," Irin remarked glumly.

From the western corridors, scores of men marched in, their weapons drawn and faces concealed behind leather helms.

"Traitors!" a familiar voice cried out. "You're very bold, Tharakk, to come here with so few."

"Commander, you survived I see." Tharakk licked his lips.

"Your insurrection has ended. Surrender. You have no other option, Tharakk."

"But I do, and surrender simply isn't what we came here to do."

A smile creased the commander's face. "I was hoping you would say that. Honestly, it wouldn't matter if you surrendered or not. The same fate awaits you either way. I just wanted to hear what you would say." Turning to his men, he said in a low voice, "Kill them."

Three more explosions shook the fort, collapsing a tower and a section of the wall. Rina lifted her arms and closed her eyes. The dust from the crumbled towers coalesced into the courtyard, hovering around the northmen. The soldiers coughed and gagged on the dust. Some frantically rubbed their eyes, trying to remove the grit, but Rina curled her fingers into a spherical shape, and the dirt and dust swirled in a vortex around the men of Dalarashess, blinding them.

Tharakk and the thworfs loosed several dozen arrows into the northmen's ranks, sowing even more confusion throughout. Some of the men cast their weapons aside and fled as best they could while shielding their faces. Screams echoed through the fort as thworf swords and arrows skewered the men of Dalarashess.

"It's working," Rina breathed excitedly.

"It isn't over yet." Tharakk motioned skyward.

A squad of six black dragons flew in from the north, unleashing torrents of fire upon the fortress, burning mostly northmen and two thworfs. Most of the thworf arrows clanked off the dragon's scales, but a few were lucky enough to pierce a wing, causing the beast to howl in rage. Swinging back around, the wounded dragon flew right for Tharakk and Rina, its red eyes shining like burning rubies. Rina reached out her right hand, but the dragon kept coming. The wizard's eyes briefly narrowed, and she tried once more. Again nothing happened, and the dragon swooped right between her and the thworf captain.

Rina dove to the side, rolling as far as she safely could, but when she lifted her head, she saw Tharakk wasn't as fortunate. The wizard looked up just as Tharakk was knocked aside. The dragon swooped back down and grabbed the hapless thworf in its jaws, thrashed him several times back and forth, and threw him against a stone wall.

"Tharakk!" Rina screamed. She focused with all her might to connect with her magic, but still her powers evaded her. Not knowing what else to do, the wizard ran over to the thworf, cradling his mangled body in her arms. "Tharakk, I'm so sorry! So, so sorry! I couldn't stop it!"

Tharakk weakly reached up and brushed his bloodied hand against Rina's cheek. "I know. You did what you could. Keep fighting. Do … do … not … let … my men … become … slave … s …" Tharakk's body collapsed, and the light faded from his eyes.

"No!" Rina howled. Clenching her jaw, she faced the northmen army. Raising her palms to the heavens, the wizard began to levitate. A tempest of green and blue fire materialized beneath her feet, spiraling upward with Rina at the core.

The dirt was sucked away and incinerated in the magic storm. Irin looked over his shoulder, and his jaw fell open. He watched without blinking as the fire tunnel continued to expand in size.

"Retreat!" Irin's voice cracked. "Fall back now!" He screamed, forcefully trying to break himself out of his enamored trance.

"Irin, what's she doing?" one of the thworfs asked.

"Something we don't want to stick around for. Come on!" Irin replied, leading the surviving thworfs out the opposite end of the courtyard and back to the woods.

The men of Dalarashess, no longer blinded, shot every arrow they could at Rina, but the arrows dissolved into ash long before they could get close to the wizard.

"Commander, what do we do?" A soldier's voice quaked.

"Kill the wizard! Kill her now!"

"How sir?"

The commander hissed in anger and thrust his sword through the soldier's chest. "Anyone else dare to question me? Kill her!"

The northmen cautiously moved toward Rina, but once the front lines came within fifty feet of the firestorm, the men evaporated. A few more arrows were fired at Rina, but to no avail. Rina screamed, and a shockwave of fire consumed everything and everyone in the courtyard. After a couple more waves, the magic detonated in a wake that overcame the entire fortress, crumbling the building to its very foundation.

# EPILOGUE
## (Six Months Later)

A fire slowly ate away at a fresh log in the fireplace. Rina stretched her toes in front of the fire, the warmth quickly thawing them. She took a swig from a nearby tankard, grabbed an old leather-bound book, and began thumbing through its pages. After another drink from the tankard, Rina heard a knock on the door. Sighing, she remained where she was and continued reading, but there was another knock, this time more forceful than before.

Rina rolled her eyes, clapped the book closed, and set it down. Pulling the door open, she irritably started, "I already told you …" Her annoyed expression quickly melted into a grin. "Irin! How did you find me? Come in, come in! Sorry, the place is a bit of a mess; I'm still settling in."

"Much better than being on the run, I can imagine."

"Yes! It's been a couple months since I encountered any of Zontose's men. "I think they have finally given up the chase, or something else more important has happened."

"The war is intensifying, Rina, and it doesn't look good. My kin have ravaged Goandria to such an extent it is hardly recognizable. We need the wizards now more than ever. My men and I could use your help, Rina."

"My help?" Rina raised her eyebrows as she took a seat on a bench next to Irin. "I'm not a wizard anymore. After I leveled that fortress, I haven't been able to connect to the blessed power. My magic is completely gone, and I cannot say I'm all that sad about it. It is nice to be normal, to not be hunted at every corner."

"Your magic has done things like that before. That doesn't mean you aren't a wizard anymore. No one can stop being a wizard."

"Yes they can, and the magic has never left for this long before. That tells me it is permanent. I'm done with fighting. What happened ..." Rina took a deep breath and choked back tears. "What happened to Tharakk was horrible. I don't want to see anyone else I care about die like that again."

Irin laid a sympathetic hand on her shoulder. "I miss him too. He knew the risks in defying Zontose. We all did, and we decided it was worth it."

"So many died that day. One by my hand."

"Ulgar wouldn't want you to blame yourself. It was an accident. He was in the very back, and the shockwave caught him. It was quick and painless. None of us blame you, Rina."

She smiled. "I know. It's just hard for me to deal with. I felt possessed by my magic, and I warned all of you that bringing me along might not be good. What's done is done, though, and we accomplished our mission."

"Yes, and Tharakk would gladly give his life for such a cause. Zontose must be stopped, and in order to do that, there will be tragedies. That is the cost of freedom, the cost of resisting evil."

Rina smiled again, her expression calm but heavy as her eyes met with the thworf's. "Thank you for all you and your men did for me. Thank you for helping me when no one else would.  If you really need my help, powers or no powers, I will be there."

Rina and Irin embraced, and in that moment, in spite of the darkness, she knew there was hope.

# Rivershore Books

www.rivershorebooks.com
blog.rivershorebooks.com
www.facebook.com/rivershore.books
www.twitter.com/rivershorebooks
Info@rivershorebooks.com

Made in the USA
Charleston, SC
12 March 2016